William Bernard MacCabe

Agnes Arnold

A novel. Part 2

William Bernard MacCabe

Agnes Arnold
A novel. Part 2

ISBN/EAN: 9783337051730

Printed in Europe, USA, Canada, Australia, Japan

Cover: Foto ©Andreas Hilbeck / pixelio.de

More available books at **www.hansebooks.com**

AGNES ARNOLD.

A NOVEL.

BY

WILLIAM BERNARD MAC CABE.

He hath found the meaning, for the which we mean
To have his head.
He must not live to trumpet forth my infamy.
PERICLES, act 1, s 1.

IN THREE VOLUMES.

VOL. II.

LONDON:
PUBLISHED BY THOMAS CAUTLEY NEWBY,
WELBECK STREET, CAVENDISH SQUARE.
MDCCCLX.

AGNES ARNOLD.

CHAPTER I.

THE UNINTENTIONAL WITNESS.

WHILST Lieutenant Kirwan Williams, and his fitting associate, Ned Reddy, were thus engaged in a long conversation, mutually interesting to themselves, and so deeply affecting the lives and fortunes of others, the widow Kinchela, true to the appointment she had made in the morning with Agnes, had travelled up from the Lodge-gate to the house.

To the widow Kinchela, all parts of Mr. Kirwan's mansion were better and longer known than to himself; for she had toddled through every room from the garret to the kitchen ten years before he was born; and her whole life, from childhood to old age, had been passed between the dwelling of the squire, and the lodge at the park-gate. It was, therefore, her custom to enter and leave the house whenever she pleased, and if, (as on the present occasion), none of the servants were in the way, to proceed to whatever room she desired. So, on reaching the house this day, she hobbled up the stairs to Miss Arnold's apartment, intending to remain there until such time as that young lady might return, and perfectly certain she would have her son Pat Kinchela—" Master John's man "—to escort her home at night.

The widow Kinchela in paying this visit to Miss Arnold was influenced by two very strong motives—affection and curiosity. She had loved Agnes as an infant; and although she had received repeated proofs of that young lady's kind remembrance of her, still Agnes was only recollected as a child, and was absolutely unknown to her as a grown-up woman, except for the few brief minutes they had conversed that morning together. The widow Kinchela wished then to disburden her old heart of all the fond, kind thoughts respecting Agnes that had been pent up in it for so many years, and that never yet had found expression in words. Therefore she was in a fever of impatience to have a long, private, and confidential conversation with the charming woman she had dandled in her arms as a baby, and whose small, weak, flute-like voice had first been taught by her to sing, with Irish words, the melodies of the country. Combined with these feelings, was another, compared with them, weak; but still sufficiently strong of itself to induce an old woman to take a long walk—and that was to see the piece of English scarlet cloth which Miss Arnold stated she had brought from England, as a special present for herself. A piece of scarlet cloth! English manufacture!— sufficiently large to make a cloak and petticoat for the winter! The widow Kinchela would not have been a woman—something better (if that is possible), or something worse (which is possible) than a woman, if she had not been impatient to see *that!*

"Ah!" said the widow Kinchela, softly opening the door of Miss Arnold's bed-chamber, and as gently closing it behind her. "Ah! the darling little girl is not here—but she has been, I see, expecting me to come to her; because there is before me, and in a place where I was sure to see it, the moment I stepped into the room, the roll of English scarlet cloth she was telling me about. The Lord cover her dainty limbs with the blessing of health, for that same Christian thought about the weak back, and the trembling limbs of an old woman!

"I wonder!" said Mrs. Kinchela, as she dropped into a chair by the side of the door, and looked at the piece of bulky red which was laid on the snow-white counterpane of the bed. "I wonder! now how many yards are there in that piece of cloth!

"I wonder is there too much or too little in it to make me a cloak and—a petticoat likewise?

"It must be very big if it can do both.

"Let me think now. How much cloth ought there to be to make me a petticoat?

"First of all, I have to consider what is the width of that cloth.

"I wonder what is the width of it!

"Some of the English manufacturers make their cloth a yard and a quarter wide, and some —my blessings on them for that same!—make it a yard and a half.

"Well, now—supposing that piece is only a

yard and quarter wide, to make me a good substantial full petticoat will require full two yards of cloth.

" I am sure, from the look of that piece, there are more than two yards, yard and a quarter wide in it.

" Yes ; that there is, and no doubt of it—so that, at all events, long life to you, Miss Arnold! I am sure of having, this next coming winter, the finest red petticoat in the parish.

" I wonder now, is there as much more cloth as will make me a cloak ?

" That requires consideration.

" I must have a hood to my cloak ; because a cloak without a hood would be like a dish of corned-beef without cabbage. For my cloak and hood I should have two yards and a half of cloth, yard and quarter wide.

" How much cloth now does all that come to ? Two yards for the petticoat—that's two ; and add to that two and a half for the cloak and hood, and it all comes to four yards and a half, a yard and quarter wide.

" I wonder are there four yards and a half, yard and quarter wide, in that piece of cloth—for if there are, it is such a beautiful flaming red, I am a made woman."

All that the widow Kinchela had to do was to step across the room, unroll the cloth, and so put an end to all her wonderings, suppositions, doubts, and calculations.   ·

The widow Kinchela knew that perfectly well ; but it was a far greater pleasure to her to sit there looking at the red cloth, and making of it a difficult problem to which her fancy might suggest twenty different solutions.   Women seem to take a peculiar delight in such like domestic riddles. Who is there that has not, in his day, observed, sometimes with amazement, and perhaps also (occasionally with impatience) a lady taking up a letter, and examining the post-marks upon it, and pondering over the seal, and trying to make out the device, or to read the motto, and at the same time " wondering *where* it came from or *who* was the writer," when all that had to be done was to remove the envelope, and so, in an instant, put an end to all guesses and surmises.

For twenty minutes and more did the widow Kinchela remain in the same position—resting her aged limbs from fatigue, and titillating her lively imagination with every description of dubiety as to the length and breadth of cloth; whilst, at the same time, she gratified her eye-sight by a contemplation of its dazzling colour.

At length she stood up, and approaching the object of her admiration as noiselessly as if it was a living creature, and she feared to disturb its repose, she laid her hand gently upon it, and rubbed it down, as if she was coaxing it.

"Ah, then," she exclaimed, "but it's it that is the fine cloth! Silk is not softer! And then, just let me feel how thick it is. Thick! It is so thick and so close, it might be raining cats and dogs for a week and a drop would not come through it. Oh, the Lord love you, my darling Miss Agnes, but this is a wonderful gift for your poor old woman!

"And now," said the widow, taking up the piece of cloth, and clasping her arms about it as fondly as if it was a baby. "What a weight it is! Four yards and a half, a yard and quarter wide! Phew! as sure as day-light, there must be a great deal more. Let me see—yes—I may as well see what is the real width of it."

The widow Kinchela replaced the cloth on the

bed, and, unfolding a small portion, she began measuring it by the length of the middle finger of her right hand—" one, two, three, four, five, six, seven, eight—now, double that, and more over! Why, as I'm a sinner, it is more than two yards wide! Well, well, well, what an old fool I am! and I, all the time sitting down on that chair—for an hour and more, I am sure—and bothering the brains out of my poor stupid head, in saying to myself, that it was no more than a yard and a quarter, and making my calculations accordingly.

"Ah, then, what length at all, at all is this two-yard wide cloth?" said the widow to herself, as she began unrolling it on the long, spacious, old-fashioned bed. "There is, I am sure, one yard and more—there are two yards and more. Why, I seem to have hardly begun it yet—it looks as if there was no end to it! Here are three yards and ——, but what is this the darling has rolled up in the centre of my bit of cloth?

"Three little cases!" cried the delighted old woman. "And all for me! I wonder what is in the inside of them! But, I may as well see! I am too impatient now to wait wondering over them. Eh! but isn't that beautiful! To think

of what would be most pleasing to me! A silver
cross with a golden image upon it! Ah, my
darling! the first thing I'll do is to have that
cross blessed by Father Murphy, and then every
morning and every night to offer up a prayer
before it—a prayer for your health here, and your
happiness hereafter. But what is the next? An
elegant, grand, silver watch, as round and thick
as a turnip! Oh, I never could wear that! That
cannot be intended for me. Ah, it is, I see, given
to me that it may be given by me to my son.
Ah, then, whoever thought they would live to see
Pat Kinchela with a silver watch in his fob? Ah,
but then isn't she the thoughtful creature thus
to have in her mind the mother and son both,
and to guess what, beyond all other things, would
make them the most happy! And now let me
see what is in the third little box. Oh, the darling
of the world! it is herself! her picture! the dead
image of what she was when she left this place to
go to England! Oh, if the Lord spares me life,
I will keep this picture, and when my darling is
married, and has lots of children, and her eldest
child that is a girl is the same age that she was
when this was taken for her, I will then give back

this same little picture to that charming little girl
that she is to have when she is the mother of a
housefull of infants. The cross I will wear next
my heart as long as life warms it. As to the
watch—here it goes into my pocket, with the
cross and picture—and it is I that will take the
rise out of Pat this evening when I give it to him,
as I am walking back with him to the Lodge.

"Oh, Kitty Kinchela! Kitty Kinchela! if
there is a happy old woman on Ireland's ground
this holy and blessed day, you are that identical
old woman!

"And now, just to see, if I am able, how
much, or about how much of cloth there is in all
this piece. I stopped reckoning at three yards
and more—here comes five yards and more. And
is it—or can it be possible? there *is*—there
actually is six yards and—a great deal more!

"Enough to fit me out with a cloak, petticoat, hood, flounces and furbelows, if I were to
make a gander of myself by wearing such fan-
dangles. Why, there is enough, aye, and more
than enough for all that with a boddice—aye—
and a shawl too to the back of it; so that if I
was to put on all at once, all the things that could

be made out of that single bit of cloth, I would walk into the chapel next Christmas-day, all in scarlet—from the top of my head to the sole of my foot, every bit of me as red as if I was a boiled lobster!

"Oh! Kitty Kinchela! it's you that are the happy woman! The Lord between us and all harm! I feel as if I was too happy!"

The widow Kinchela stopped suddenly in the midst of her exultation; for she heard, or fancied she heard, the tread of two men's feet, as if they were mounting stealthily the stairs which led to the study of Mr. Kirwan and bed-room of Miss Arnold, as they were adjoining each other on the same floor.

The widow Kinchela listened and trembled!

"The Lord preserve us!" said Mrs. Kinchela, dropping the cloth which she had again rolled up on the bed. "What is the meaning of this? The master and all the family are out! There are none but women-servants in the house. And these—whoever they are—are creeping stealthily up the stairs! And now—they are in the passage outside! And now—they are coming—coming along towards this room! What is

going to happen at all? Ah! they are now outside the door of the master's study. That is
always locked when he is out."

The widow Kinchela listened and she distinctly heard these words spoken in a whispering
voice :—

"Give me the keys? You know no more the
proper use to make of them than I do of trigo-
nometry or mensuration. There is a knack
about them, as well as in coining, and all other
arts for making money easy. See there! one
twist with this little fellow—and you have a door
as ready to your bidding as a dog to run after his
master. I follow you, sir. Just give me a hint
where you think the old fellow's money is hidden,
and I'll have it out, and in your hands before
you could reckon twenty."

The voice ceased, and the widow Kinchela
heard the door of Mr. Kirwan's study closed.

The old woman fell on her knees, offered up
a fervent, heart-broken prayer, and then rising
up, she thus communed with herself :—

"Thieves! there are thieves—two thieves in
the master's study! Two men! and none but
women in the house! If I give the alarm—if I

screech out, it will be of no use. I shall be murdered, and all that the poor girls that hear me can
do will be to come up and get murdered along
with me !

" The Lord look down and pity me this
day ! What am I to do, at all, at all ?

" If I attempt to creep out of this room, they
will hear me passing the door, for thieves are
always on the watch, like a cat; and they will
think no more of trampling the life out of me
than if I was a frog !

" What then in the world am I to do ?

" To hide myself here.

" Easy said, but where am I to hide myself?

" Oh, dear ! oh, dear ! but had'nt I the hard
luck to come here to-day ? Wasn't it for my
death I put on my clean best cap when I left
my own humble little cottage this morning?

" Oh ! Kitty Kinchela ! Kitty Kinchela ! if
there is an unhappy, heart-broken, desolate
creature in all the whole, wide, universal world—
the Lord pity you !—but it's you that are that
most miserable old woman this day !

" Oh ! the villains ! the villains ! I can hear
them dragging at drawers, and pulling open

presses; and it's they that are, I engage, filling
their pockets with gold.   Little good may it do
to them the murdering robbers !

"May be, they will find more than they can
carry with them in that room, and will never
think of coming into this.

"But if they do—what is to become of me
at all, at all; or where am I to hide myself?

"There isn't a trunk in the room big enough to
hold me.   And if there was they would be sure to
open it, and rob me of my life, my golden crucifix,
Pat's silver watch, and Miss Arnold's picture.

"The presses too are locked; and if they
were not, the thieves would be sure to find me
hiding in them, and then there would be an end
—and a miserable cut-throat end also, to poor
old Kitty Kinchela."

The widow Kinchela looked anxiously around
the room, and then suddenly said :—

"Ah ! Heaven in its mercy has heard my
prayer !   There is one chance—a very poor
chance for me—even if they do come into the
room.

"Here," said the widow Kinchela, as she
crept along the narrow space or passage that in

all old-fashioned bed-chambers lay between the bed and the wall, and which is so frequently referred to in the French fashionable writers of the seventeenth and eighteenth centuries as the *ruelle*. " Here," she said, creeping up this narrow passage, and opening the thick heavy folds of the long, rich damask curtains which were gathered around the head of the bed, and fell from its roofing to the floor. " Here! " she sighed, as she wrapped their folds around her, and so stood up completely concealed from observation—" here is the last and only chance for my life. I am safe, unless they take to stealing the curtains—but if they do—the Lord have mercy on me! for I never shall see daylight again."

So stood cold, pale, silent and trembling the poor old widow Kinchela, and thus she determined to remain until she heard the sound of the carriage-wheels, and the noise of the accompanying cavalcade upon the return, at night, of Mr. Kirwan and Miss Arnold.

Meanwhile, the Lieutenant and his associate were busily occupied. For an entire hour, they had been labouring with unceasing activity. At the end of that time Ned Reddy turned to the Lieutenant, and said:—" Is there any other place in the room you can think of, Master James ? "

The Lieutenant cast a despairing look at the sides, at the ceiling, and at last upon the floor, and then with a deep sigh, or rather groan, he responded :—" None ! none ! none ! We have tried all."

" Hum ! " said Ned Reddy, " That is the most impossible thing that ever I knew to be possible in all my born experience of such matters. To be in a room that you know is full of money, and yet not to be able to find a farthing beyond something like a hundred one pound notes of Beresford's bank in what is, plainly on the face of it, his strong box, and that little sum only kept there for what may be con- sidered every day use. Never since the world was a world was there ever anything like to that."

" It is incomprehensible to me," said the Lieutenant, " for I heard him with my own ears tell Miss Arnold her deeds and her bank receipts were in this room—the room we are now stand-

ing in—and as we have not been able to come
upon the slightest trace of them, we may well
believe that wherever her property is concealed
his money is along with it."

"Then where are they—if they are in this
very room?" asked Reddy, impatiently.

"Ah! Ned, Ned!" replied the Lieutenant,
"I would willingly give the four thousand you
were asking for, to be able to answer that
question."

"Listen to him!" said Reddy bitterly.
"When he thought he could lay his hands on the
money he was for making a hard bargain with
me; but now that there is little chance of his
having more than a hundred pounds for his pains,
he is for giving away thousands! Ah! there is
—it is plain from that—the genteel drop in your
heart, notwithstanding the mother's colour on
your cheek, Master James."

"This is no time for taunts or reproaches,"
replied the Lieutenant. "I am a greater loser
than you by the disappointment."

"I don't know that, Master James," answered
Reddy, sulkily. "It is just possible that you
are all this time bamboozling me. You were not

at first, very well disposed to let me join in over-hauling your uncle's study; and now, that you have appeared to consent to let me do so, it may be that you are blind-folding me—opening every-thing for me—showing me everything, but still keeping away from me the only one thing material —that is, the place where all the money is con-cealed."

"Your suspicions are unjust, Reddy. That is all I can say," answered the dispirited Lieute-nant. "You have asked me, if I knew of any other place where we could search for the money. I now ask you the same question. Look well and carefully around you. You boasted of your skill and experience in these matters. You said you could smell out money wherever it was con-cealed. Put forth then all your ability. See, if you can discover the hiding-place. I hope you may be successful."

"Plainly spoken enough," answered Reddy, "and I own I am more inclined to believe you mean me fairly, by talking in this way, than if you had bounced out in a passion, when I charged you with trying to cheat me."

The walls were carefully searched anew—the

floor was struck, to see if there was any hollow sound—the chimney-piece and hearth-stone were again re-examined, the presses again re-opened, the drawers in every table again ransacked, and the result was the same—the treasures of Mr. Kirwan remained undiscoverable.

"I give it up! I am dead beat—beat like a hack!" said Reddy. "There is no use in losing any more time to-day in seeking for what is unapproachable—for what, I believe, will never be come-at-able until you are the master of this house, and poor Mr. Kirwan's keys in your possession. Ah, if I had but the examination of those keys for one quarter of an hour, I could soon pick the way to the secret. I would soon know, from that, where was the particular hiding place the money was kept. Now, however, and without such a clue, I am dead beat, and I admit it. So, good-bye, Master James, I am off for Turview, in order that I may be the first to bring you back, as I hope, all the good news you expect."

"Do—do," said the Lieutenant. "Be the first to convey the good news. Tell me that my uncle is arrested, and I will give you forty pounds:

tell me that Miss Arnold's abduction is effected, and I will give you thirty pounds more : tell me that John has been killed in resisting the arrest, or trying to prevent the abduction, and you shall have another thirty pounds."

" Why, Master James, if you give me all that you will break your uncle's bank of all its one pound Beresford notes. But, come, I will try for them. Pay, or no pay, you shall, be it good or bad, have the first news at all events, or I shall break my heart in running."

The widow Kinchela, in her place of conceal-ment, heard the two men parting outside Miss Arnold's door. She listened to the stealthy steps of one as he departed; and then, to her horror, she beheld the other opening the door, and doubly locking it behind him. It was with difficulty she suppressed an exclamation of terror, surprise, and grief, when she recognised, in the face of the intruder, the well-known features of James—the nephew of her beloved master !

Trembling from fear, she observed written in that frowning, frigid, and cruel countenance, open manifestations of the base acts which had been already accomplished in the adjoining room, and that were now about to be completed in her presence.

She saw her master's nephew look cautiously and earnestly around all parts of the room, as if he surmised, or feared there might be a looker-on ; and then she perceived him draw forth a bunch of skeleton-keys, and apply one to the largest of the lady's trunks. The top of the trunk flew wide open—the felon glanced at its contents, but for an instant, shut down the cover, and relocked it.

"Psha!" he cried, "ladies dresses! what have I to do with such gew-gaws and trumpery? I suppose it is the same with them all. Let me try this chest of drawers."

The skeleton keys were again used. In an instant, the sharp clicking of the bolts, as they were rapidly shot back one after another, was heard, and the drawers were, in succession, quickly opened.

"What, dresses! and again dresses!" he sneeringly remarked. "What creatures these women are! They never think they can be sufficiently disguised with decorations! And for what purpose? To attract our notice—to win our love—and then to laugh at us for our admira-

tion of them; to despise us for being so easily
entrapped! Ah, women's love is not my weakness.
Give me wealth! give me power! give me high
rank! These, too, are what women desire; and
the man who possesses such gifts, though foul as
a satyr, and low-born as the basest churl, is sure
to command their affections. Here, now, are
laces, ribbons, scents, powders, patches, and—I
know not even by name—what other vile stuffs
besides. These are not what I seek. I shall not
vex myself by looking further into them."

Again the drawers were closed as rapidly as
they had been opened.

Lieutenant Williams stopped for a moment,
and again cast a sharp and scrutinizing glance
around the room.

"Am I doomed?" he said, for so certain was
he that he was quite alone in the large, wide
mansion, that he spoke his thoughts aloud: "Am
I doomed to be, this day, disappointed in everything? I have missed what I sought for in the
adjoining room. Does a similar disappointment
await me here? Agnes has not yet had time to
arrange the various articles that belong to her.
Where, then, can be her writing-desk? I fancied

I could at once lay my hands upon it. Let me see—in which of those trunks is it most possible I shall find it? Ah! there!—there is a square wooden-box. Perhaps that contains the casket, in which I may find all the damsel's secrets."

He knelt down by the side of the wooden-box, again applied a skeleton key to the lock, and, with one hand, held up the lid, and then flinging it back, exclaimed, with a joyful shout :—

"I have it! I have it! Ha! now Agnes Arnold, you are for ever in my power—for ever, henceforth—my abject slave!"

"Ah, me!" sighed the widow Kinchela, incapable for the instant of repressing her horror, whilst listening to the felon's demoniacal shout of joy, and the vile threat with which it was accompanied.

As the half-murmured sigh reached his ears, the Lieutenant let fall the lid of the box—a cold thrill of fear ran through his veins, and starting up, he drew forth a long dagger, and asked, in a voice that trembled with terror :—

"Who's there? who calls? Any one outside the door?"

There was no answer given to these questions.

There was a dead, dull silence in the room. Not a stir was audible; but, as the widow Kinchela looked through the thick damask curtains, she could dimly discern a whitish face a short distance from her—the corpse-like, distorted visage of the Lieutenant—whilst she felt her own heart beat so strongly in her bosom, that she feared its violent throbbings would reveal her hiding-place.

"I cannot be mistaken," continued the Lieutenant, still speaking aloud. "I heard the words, 'Ah, me!' spoken plainly and distinctly.

"There is some one in this room!

"I know there is!

"Let that person—be it man or woman—at once tell me where they are, and they are forgiven. Let them continue to try and hide themselves, and so sure as they are now listening to me, I will plunge this dagger up to the very hilt, in their hearts.

"Come forth, I say, at once! Come forth! or you have not five minutes more to live.

"The spy will not do so: the skulker refuses to stir!

"Now, then, to search: I will not leave a corner of the apartment unvisited by my dagger's point."

True to his word, the felon's keys unlocked every press and wardrobe, and every trunk, capable of containing any living thing, was opened, and pierced venomously with his dagger.

Tired out with his useless search, the Lieutenant stopped in the centre of the room, and looked again around. There was not visible, to his eye, the appearance of anything capable of concealing a human being.

"There is no one here!" he said, in amazement, "and yet, I heard words spoken that were not my own! How can that be?

"Might it not be the wind? some sudden whiff of air penetrating through a key-hole or chink, which my excited fancy has mistaken for those two words—'Ah, me!'—that sounded in my ears as distinctly as any words I ever heard spoken.

"But, come what may, I must now coplete the task that I have begun."

The Lieutenant lifted the box from the floor to a table. He then took out the writing-desk, and opening it, observed it was filled with correspondence of various kinds.

"Ha!" he exclaimed, "now to master the

young lady's sweet thoughts : now to have a clue
to all her actions. Here are some hours' occupa-
tion. It is well I have brought a light with me."

Deliberately and methodically, the Lieutenant
set to work. Daylight sank into darkness, and
then the solitary lamp was lighted, and, by its
dim beams, the trembling old woman could
indistinctly discern, as each package was laid
aside, the blank look of disappointment portrayed
in the face of the reader, whilst such exclamations
as these came, as it were, involuntarily from his
lips :—

"Nonsense! all nonsense!   School-girls'
friendships!—moonlight and everlasting affection!
What is all this I have been reading ?   ' *Letters
from dear Papa !*' Balderdash! ' *Memorials of
poor, dear Mama !*' Fudge! ' *Correspondence
with good Mr. Kirwan.*' Humbug! And—eh!
what is this ? Poetry! Ah, there should be
something suggestive here. Bah! extracts from
Milton — Thompson — Akenside— Shenstone—
Goldsmith—a set of fools, who never wrote one
ardent love-sonnet, with all their scribbling.
There is not here a single amorous line. No—
not even a vulgar valentine, with bleeding hearts

and fiery arrows! Nothing—nothing—nothing wherewith to annoy, or thwart, or reproach her!

"Oh, by my life!" said the Lieutenant, as he bounded up from his chair, "I am wrong! Ha! ha! Miss Agnes! found out at last! Who, I should wish to know, is *this* the miniature of? Upon my word, a fine, handsome, smiling Lothario! a coaxing, dashing, rattling, young cavalry officer! Ha! this tell-tale portrait is enough for me. I will take the liberty of retaining this for my own use—hereafter. Now, my pert, saucy, young jade, I have, in this small bit of ivory, an instrument wherewith to break your proud heart!"

"Oh!" groaned forth the poor old woman, paralysed with terror at these threats against her beloved Agnes.

"Ha! skulking listener! whoever you are, now I have caught you. Now I will slay you like a dog, now I know you are in this room, and I shall never cease till I discover you;" said the desperate villain, as he again clutched his dagger, and again ran about the chamber furiously thrusting it into the bed, and then behind all the chairs.

" No one to be found ! " he ejaculated, as he
suddenly stopped, and dropped the dagger on the
table.   " Is this madness or fear on my part ?

" It is a mystery beyond my comprehension.
I have, however, found all that I wished for. The
means whereby I can make Agnes fawn like a
spaniel at my feet.   And now to replace the
papers as I found them—and then—to await the
joyful tidings which the Red Spy is sure to bring
me. Yes, the estate will be mine, with no brother
to share it ; and Agnes, too, shall be mine, with
no brother, nor nameless English officer to be
dreaded as a rival.   All ! all smiles upon me !
My success is certain."

So speaking, the Lieutenant closed the door
as he left the room ; and as his retreating steps
were heard, the nerves of the poor, terrified old
woman relaxed from the tension in which they
had been held for so many hours, and she fell,
with a convulsive groan, senseless on the floor.

CHAPTER II.

ENGLAND AND IRELAND—CONTEM-
PLATED UNION!

IT was one of the arrangements consequent upon
the wounds received by John Kirwan Williams that
the family carriage should be reserved for himself
and the physician. The other occupants of Mr.
Kirwan's carriage (when travelling to Turview)
were thus distributed for the purpose of returning—Mr. Kirwan and his ward, Miss Arnold, in
a post-chaise—whilst Miss Arnold's maid was
confided to the care of a tall, well-looking, young
servant named Patrick Kinchela, (the son of the
widow Kinchela) and the favourite as well as
confidential attendant of the young barrister.

The charge confided to Patrick Kinchela was
willingly undertaken, and the spirit in which it
was desired to be performed was indicated in the
first words he addressed to Lucy.

"We have an old proverb in Ireland, Miss,

which, as you labour under the awful misfortune
of not being able to talk Irish, I may as well say
to you in English ; and it is this—' What is one
man's meat is another man's poison ;' or, in other
words, ' what is a misfortune with one person
may be the top of good luck to another.' That
is the case this blessed night with my poor young
master and myself. If he had not been so
unlucky as to get into a scrimmage with a pack
of thieving Orangemen, and so obliged to keep
all the coach to himself and the apothecary, then
poor Pat Kinchela would be riding home all
alone and dreary by himself, instead of having
the mighty great happiness of taking care of such
a lovely girl as yourself, and the still greater
happiness of having you riding on a pillion
behind him ; and that which is next door to the
very height of all happiness—that is being
married to you—feeling one of your dawney
hands and elegant-shaped arms around me for so
many miles of the road."

"Pon my word ! Mr. Kinchela, I am very
much obliged to you for saying that. Pray, tell
me—for I am a stranger in the country—are all
young Irishmen as polite as yourself ? "

" I do not very well know what you mean by being polite," answered Kinchela; " but if your signification of politeness is—admiring a pretty girl when one sees her, and because she is pretty wishing to do everything on earth to oblige her; then, in that case—all Irishmen—rich and poor, old and young, gentle and simple—are made up of nothing in the world but politeness."

" Ah !" said Lucy, smiling,—" I see, Mr. Kinchela, you are a very strange people, and it is very hard for us English folk to understand you."

" True for you !" answered Kinchela. " The English do find it very hard to understand us, and the reason is, they never try to understand us. They have their peculiarities ; we have ours ; they think all ours is nonsense, and all their own perfect reason ; and, therefore no matter how we may feel, or what we may think on subjects most clear to ourselves, all such, our notions, are contemned by them, and they are for forcing their ideas or their customs upon us, no matter whether we like them or not."

" I can only speak for myself, Mr. Kinchela," replied Lucy, " I merely remark on what I have myself observed. I say—I do not understand *the Irish*—perhaps, what I ought to have said, is—I do not understand *you.*"

"Not understand *me!* Perhaps I do not speak plain English," replied Kinchela. "Now, if I was to say to you, that I think you one of the very handsomest girls ever I saw, and that I would sooner be married to you, than to snuffy old Queen Charlotte on the throne of England, would you understand me?"

"That is not plain English," said Lucy again laughing—" that is downright nonsense; and you know it is, Mr. Kinchela. You are only bantering me as if I was a silly, little girl of sixteen."

" Is it *I* banter a sensible young woman? Oh, no!—Miss Lucy—that may be the fashion with your countrymen; but an Irishman, giddy as you may think him, has the sense to know beauty when he sees it, and he has too much respect for it to make game of it."

" I see you are incorrigible, Mr. Kinchela— but still I must remark, from what I have observed of your conduct this whole evening, that I cannot understand you—and the reason, I suppose I cannot do so is—because you are an Irishman."

"Explain yourself, Miss Lucy, if you please," said Kinchela; "for if I understand you right, I don't know what you mean."

"Very well, Mr. Kinchela, as you wish it, I shall endeavour to explain my meaning. Here now are you, Mr. Kinchela riding before me, talking —I beg your pardon for saying it—the softest nonsense !—and that too in a voice as gentle as a child ; so that one to listen to you, as you now have been speaking to me, would suppose that your temper was so angelic, and your disposition so meek that no possible event in this world could ever disturb your tranquillity. Now then, Mr. Kinchela what I cannot understand about you— looking at you as you appear this instant—how is it possible that you can be the same person that—it is not two hours since I am certain—I saw raging like a madman about the barn when you found your young master wounded !— flourishing a dragoon's sword around your head ! and calling out, 'for the face of an Orangeman,' in order that you might, without more ado, chop his head off!—I do not like to repeat the horrid word you used in connection with the decapitated head of an Orangeman! And then, Mr. Pat Kinchela, I remember remarking you—when you could find nobody to fight with—in the madness of your rage cutting down whole branches of candlesticks, and knocking the lighted tops off unoffending candles! These sudden changes, Mr. Kinchela, are incomprehensible to me. I cannot, I say, understand how the self-same person can be blustering about like a rude *Boreas ;* and then—all of a sudden—in less than an hour afterwards, be as gentle, and as soft-voiced as if he had been playing nothing but *Cupid* all his life! Now, Mr. Kinchela, do you comprehend what I wish to say when I declare that I— as an Englishwoman—am not merely astonished, but bewildered at these varieties in the Irish character!"

"Partly, I understand you, miss," quietly answered Kinchela, "and it is probable I could understand you better if you did not use such hard words. I cannot say, that I am quite sure who *Boreas* was—but I suppose, some hulking, ill-conditioned fellow, that went about the world, always making as much noise as if he was screeching drunk. As to *Cupid*, every fool, of course, has heard of him, as being what they call 'the god of love.' And now, Miss Lucy, to come to your question—you say, you cannot understand how I, that am speaking to you here, as a young man should speak to a young woman—that is to a very well-looking young woman—could possibly be the same person that you describe as in a raging passion cutting mould-six candles into mould-fours, because he could find nobody to fight with him. Isn't that the matter—because you are an Englishwoman and I am an Irishman—you want to have explained to you."

" Yes—yes—precisely," replied Lucy. " I want to know what is your real character. Are you a wicked or a quiet person? I want to know whether you were serious then, or whether you are in earnest now? "

" My real character, and the character of every other real Irishman is to be *in earnest*, whatever he is doing," answered Kinchela. " We all hate to be disappointed. If we are in for a fight, we do not like to part from one another until we have had a fight. If we are for making love, we do not like to part from the girl of our heart, until she has not only said 'yes,' but is also not unwilling to hear the day named for her marriage. You say, I am not like the same person I was an hour or two ago. To be sure I am not. I would be ashamed of myself, if I was. A pretty thing, indeed! it would be, if, when the care of such a little darling as you are was given to me, and when I got you on horseback behind me, I went roaring at you like a giant, and frightening you with my frowns, and terrifying you with my curses! Would you expect that conduct from me? Is there living an Englishman, you think, who could so behave to you? If there is—you ought to be ashamed of your country! And if that would not be proper in an Englishman— in what way is it strange to you, that it would be proper in an Irishman? And then—my behaviour awhile ago, when you say I was like a madman. Well, now, what in the world could be more reasonable than that I should be like a madman, when I saw my darling young master —brave young Kirwan—a real Kirwan, stretched for dead and—all for what?—because he was trying to save your young mistress from being run away with by that tall, ungainly, ugly, ill-looking, 'walking-gallows,' Captain Hepenstall! would you expect me at such a time as that to be like a little school-girl, and bowing, and smiling, and making my *gulluthus* to everybody I met, and saying, ' Please sir! who did *this?* ' and 'please ma'am! how has all *that* happened?' and, 'what's the name of the polite gentleman who has murdered my young master?' If you say, that is the way an Englishman would act under such circumstances, all I say again is Miss Lucy—you ought to be ashamed of your country."

"But then, Mr. Kinchela—you Irish appear to be so ready to fight with one another, and at the same time so prompt, or perhaps I ought to say—hasty—in making love. I judge of others by you."

"Thank you! for the compliment, Miss Lucy. But you are right. I am a fair sample of an every-day Irishman. And you say we are so ready to fight, and so hasty in making love. Well—you are right again. There is no real fighting without love; and no real love without fighting."

"Then you make fighting and love the same thing!"

"To be sure I do. No man is worth a
trawneen in making love, who is not ready to
have his full share in a fight; and take my
word for it, Miss Lucy, that the fellow who
makes love to you, and would not be prepared to
fight to the death, sooner than let any other
blackguard insult, annoy, or molest you is a
skulking, scheming, good-for-nothing, milksop,
that it would be much better for you to have
nothing to do with—for it is a common remark
in Ireland, 'that it is only the coward and the
poltroon amongst men that is a tyrant at home,
that beats his wife, and *harishes* the children.'"

"Ah! Mr. Kinchela, you have not answered
my objection."

"What is it, Miss Lucy?"

"The readiness of the Irish to fight with one
another—and then your being—as it seems to
me—as well pleased with fighting as with love-
making."

"Well now, Miss Lucy, as to your first objection, we are not ready to fight with one another;
but we are ready to resent an unprovoked insult,
and we are ready to repel an unjustifiable wrong.
If an ill-behaved fellow gets into Irish company,

and has no one to back him, he is kicked out at once, and there is an end of him, and—there is no fighting; but, if he has a faction behind him who haven't time to stop and listen to reason, then there is, I admit, very apt to be a fight—but then, you see, it all arises from the very best motive in the world—the dislike an Irishman has to see one that is a friend overborne by numbers, no matter whether he is in the right or wrong. It is not fair then, Miss Lucy, to say the Irish are ready to fight with one another."

"Dear me! Mr. Kinchela—you astonish me to hear you say so—when I have seen this very night such frightful outrages committed, and all on account of the playing of a mere tune, which if played in England no one would have thought either of applauding or censuring."

"There! you English go again!" answered the undaunted Kinchela.—"Judging of what happens in Ireland by what is customary in England. Why, there are, Miss Lucy, some *tunes* in Ireland that are ' *war-cries?* ' They are played, not for amusement, but to provoke men to fight, because though the airs themselves are nothing but sounds in music, they are played for

the purpose of telling those who listen to them—
'you are slaves—you are beaten slaves—our
fathers' cut your fathers' throats, and we wish to
cut yours, and will do so *now*, if you dare but to
show the slightest resentment—and if you do not
exhibit any resentment, then it is because you
are cowards, runaways, poltroons.' Now, Miss
Lucy, I am no historian nor politician, but this I
can tell you that when the whole of the Saxon
nation, kings, nobles, priests, and people were
overthrown in a scrimmage called ' the battle of
Hastings,' by a pack of robbing, plundering,
murdering, Norman-Frenchmen, it is said, that
the great fight in which the English were overthrown was begun by a Norman-fiddler playing
up a tune called 'the Song of Roland.' Now,
supposing, Miss Lucy, the Normans not content
with robbing and plundering the Saxon nation
were always, for the purpose of insulting and
provoking the people, and reminding them of the
battle of Hastings, and all the dismal murders
and spoliations that followed it to their loss and
degradation, for ever dinning that tune of ' the
Song of Roland ' into the ears of the English—
do you think that the English people, knowing it

was played to insult and cock-crow over them, would have kept on never minding it—would have laughed at their being insulted—would have applauded the musicians, and would have looked on the Normans and their fiddlers as friends for playing it? If they would—then all I can say is they would deserve to be spit upon as rascally mean-spirited, skulking Saxon slaves, instead of being respected as they rightly are as ' free-born Englishmen ;' and you ought, if your Saxon ancestors had been so insulted, and so patiently submitted to their Norman masters, to be ashamed of your country. But, the fact is, Miss Lucy, that things have happened in Ireland, the like of which never occurred in England, and the consequence is that when the English pass judgment upon us, they do so under the great disadvantage of knowing nothing at all of our past history, and in being sedulously misinformed as to our present condition."

" I declare, Mr. Kinchela, you quite surprise me with your knowledge and observations—but still—excuse me for pressing you on the point—you have given me no explanation—of the horrid scene of to-night—the readiness with which you

Irish, rushed into the conflict with each other.
The Irish, on both sides, seemed to me eager to
engage in deadly strife."

"And is it really possible," said Kinchela
stopping his horse, in order that he might with
the more ease turn round on his saddle and look
his fair companion in the face. "Did you
actually," said he, raising his eye-brows, as in
amazement : "Could you truly have believed
that they were Irishmen on both sides, in that
battle of to-night ? "

"Undoubtedly I did. What were they but
Irish, on both sides ? " replied Lucy.

"Oh! well! after that! there is no use in
talking! Go on with you—you *omadhaun*! "
said Kinchela, as he gave a slight touch with his
whip to the horse. "Oh! after saying that! the
sooner I bring this journey to an end the better.
Why, my charming, darling, blue-eyed beauty."

"Don't use such strong language, if you
please, Mr. Kinchela."

"I cannot help it, my love of the world! my
heart is so full of grief at seeing the delusion you
are labouring under, that I have not the strength
of mind to pay proper attention to the expressions

I am using. When a man is in grief he always says what he thinks. And so you say *cushlama-chree!* that you believe—still believe you saw two parties of Irishmen fighting through one another, in the barn that was fitted up as a ball-room ? "

" If they were not all Irishmen, Mr. Kinchela, what were they ? "

" Well—I'll make it plain to you—as plain as the pretty nose between the sparkling blue eyes on your own sweet, lovely face. Are you, Miss Lucy, an Irishwoman, because you are riding on an Irish horse ? "

" No, Mr. Kinchela. The mere accident of riding on an Irish horse cannot, most assuredly, entitle me to call myself an Irishwoman."

" Very well, then—no more does the riding rough-shod over Ireland make a pack of foreign vagabonds, Irishmen. You say there were two parties of Irishmen fighting in the ball-room. I say there was *only one party of Irishmen,* and at the head of *that party* was my poor, young master—Kirwan Williams, who is now lying on the broad of his back in the master's carriage before us, and bleeding like a pig from the wounds he got from *the other party.*"

" And what do you call the other party, Mr. Kinchela ? "

" The *English* party, to be sure," stoutly replied Kinchela.

" The *English* party !   Oh ! Mr. Kinchela, I am quite ashamed of you !   How *can* you say there was an English party there, when the only person in the room, a native of England, was myself? "

" Ah ! then, Miss Lucy, it is you, I engage that can see a hole through a ladder with those eyes of yours, that are just like two new-born violets changing into diamonds.   What was *the colour* of the coats worn by the *other party* that tried to make mince-meat of my master with their sabres?   Did not Hepenstall wear a red coat, and did'nt Keogh and the other vagabonds wear blue coats with orange facings?   Are not those, Miss Lucy, the colours of *the English* infantry and cavalry,—*red* for the one, and *blue* for the other.   Green, Miss Lucy—grass—bright *grass green* is the colour of *Ireland*, and that you might have seen worn by one or two that were fighting by the side of the young master.   A man's *party* is known by his *colours ;* and there-

fore I say that of the parties that were fighting
this night—the one was an *English,* and the other
an *Irish* party. And now, having settled that
matter as plain as two and two make four, I
would like, if you have no objection, just to make
one remark, because it will be answering a question you asked me awhile ago, and that I dis-
remembered until this minute."

"Go on Mr. Kinchela, I am listening to you
with pleasure."

"My blessings on you! my little band-box
of beauty for saying so. Well, now, the one
remark I have to make is—But before I say
another word, just clasp your darling arm a little
tighter round me ; for we are coming to a very
rough part of the road, hereabouts—and if you
don't hold a firm grip of me, and the horse was
to stumble some horrid frightful accident might
happen to you. Aye—that's it—that is the right
way to grasp me, if you wish to save yourself
from a fall. Well, now then listen to the
remark I have to make—or, rather the plain question I have to ask you. It is this. Could anything
be going on nicer, nor pleasanter, nor happier,
nor more agreeable than the dance we had in the

barn, until Hepenstall and his faction came among us?"

"No—nothing indeed," replied Lucy. "All was good temper and merriment, and I was enjoying myself exceedingly."

"See that now! oh! if you—the good-natured, honest-hearted English—would only judge of us fairly with your own eyes, how much happier should we two nations be together! Well now, Miss Lucy, as sure as you and I are now riding on the same horse—that is the harmless, harmonious way we—I mean the Irish—would go on for ever, if we were only let alone. But we won't be let alone—we won't be let to be at peace with each other, because there is a set of schemers amongst us, (some pretending to be 'patriots,' more saying they are 'Orangemen,')—whose interest it is to misrepresent us, and to misdescribe us as being 'disloyal,' or 'turbulent,' or 'discontented,' or 'incorrigible,' or 'always disposed to be fighting'—and these vagabonds when they find we are quiet, and not behaving ourselves in a way that would make that appear to be true which they say of us, they then break in amongst us, perhaps to incite us to fight, perhaps to maltreat us, perhaps to compel us, in our own defence to give them, or those who are in their pay, or under their orders, an uncommon good leathering, just as we did to-night—more of that to them, and worse luck to them, the thieves of the universe."

" I declare, Mr. Kinchela, I think you are quite right. Upon reflection, I am convinced there would not have been the slightest disturbance in the ball-room if those very badly behaved persons had not intruded upon you in the first instance, and grossly misconducted themselves afterwards."

" It is easy seeing, my enchanting rose-bud, that you are a rock of sense," said the insinuating Kinchela. " Why, if those fellows had staid away, instead of my sitting, like an ill-behaved man, that is, with my back turned to the prettiest girl in all Wexford, I might be this minute facing you in a reel, ' turning corners' instead of turning out on the high road, and ' crossing hands,' instead of crossing ditches. High hanging to them! the Tories! Only for them, you and I might be about this time capering away to the only tune I would ever wish to hear you call for."

" What tune may that be, Mr. Kinchela ? "

"'*Haste to the wedding,*' my honey-bee," replied the enamoured Kinchela.

"Well, really! Mr. Kinchela, I do not know what to say to you; but you strive to make yourself very interesting and amusing."

"Ah, then, how is it possible for me to be either the one or the other, with my countenance turned away from you, as if you were as ugly as sin, and as old as my grandmother. No man can possibly be amusing or interesting to a a girl, when it's with his back he is looking at her. But, I wouldn't care so much for that, if those thieves had only kept away one hour longer —for I was to have danced—and that too at the particular desire of the old master—the 'polthering jig '—and there was to have been brought in a door into the middle of the barn, for me to have danced it. Oh, my lovely white-rose of sweetness, if *you* had but seen me dance that dance—then, indeed, you might say that I could be both interesting and amusing."

"Oh, then you are proud of your dancing?"

"Is it me? proud! not a bit in life, my darling duck of diamonds!"

"Not of your dancing generally; but of that

particular dance with the unpronouncable name,"
said Lucy.

"You mean the 'polthering jig.' No, I am
not proud of that neither, but this I will say—
give me a good door—well and smoothly laid to
dance upon, with a little hollow in the floor, so that
what I do may be fairly and well seen—give me
with that, an active fiddler, half drunk, so that he
would never lag in playing up to me with the
proper spirit—that is, a spirit equal to my own—
and then let us have fair play together, and all I
will venture to remark about myself is this—that
there is not a man nor a boy from eighteen to
twenty-eight years old, in the thirty-two counties
of Ireland, that could match me in the 'polthering
jig.' Why, Miss Lucy, I declare to you—it is as
true, as that I am already over head and ears in
love with you—there are six steps of my own
invention in that one jig; and when I am dancing
them—that is, on a well-laid door, with a souple-
elbowed fiddler to help me out—I kick up such
a clatter, you would swear you heard twenty
drum-boys, in a marching regiment, all beating
away together and seeing which should be able
to make the most noise. And now to think of

it ! Is it not enough to drive a man mad ? Only
for the villains that interrupted us, I should have
had the opportunity of dancing that very jig—
and with you, my heart's delight, looking on at
me ! That I may never be united in the bonds
of holy matrimony with the girl I most admire,
but I believe if I had *you* looking at me in that
jig, I would get so full of fun, frisk, frolic, joy,
and spirit, that I would never stop dancing on
the door, until I had knocked it all—panels, bolts,
bars, and hinges into little chips, splinters, and
sparables."

"I am beginning to be afraid, the more I
listen to you, Mr. Kinchela," said the sly and
highly-pleased Lucy, " that you are too much of
an enthusiast."

"An enthusiast! not I," replied Kinchela,
" unless it be an enthusiast to be in downright
earnest, whatever you are doing—dancing on a
door, fighting with a rascal, or making love to a
pretty girl. And that now, Miss Lucy, brings me
to an answer I wished to give to a question you
put to me a while ago."

"Dear me ! Mr. Kinchela, you surprise me !

I never asked you a question about your love-making, I am sure," tartly replied Lucy.

"Oh, certainly not," quickly retorted Kinchela, "but you asked me this, or, at all events, something like it. Whether the Irish were as well pleased to be engaged in fighting as in love-making?"

"Yes, yes, I said that from the readiness you shewed to rush into either extreme—from one to the other—that it was doubtful which was the more agreeable to you."

"Well, then, from this day forth, make your mind perfectly easy on that point," replied Kinchela. "There is nothing in all this wide world that would be half so pleasing to myself as to be making love to you—"

"Stop, stop, stop! Mr. Kinchela, I really cannot listen to you," said Lucy, relaxing her hold on her conductor's coat.

"You may close both your ears with one hand, if you like," said Kinchela, "but don't, for your life, let go your grip of me with the other, or you may fall off the horse. I am a plain-spoken boy, Miss Lucy, and what I am going to say to you is not what you, may be, expect to hear; but, at all

D 2

events, it is the truth. Now, I repeat it, I would
sooner be making love to you than to be the
Emperor of Germany.   But, what do I mean by
making love ? Is it paying you empty compli-
ments, and saying all those fine things that are said
of great beauties in street ballads, sung in Wexford
town on a market day, calling you a Venus, and
a Juno, or an Andromache, or a Hecuba, or a
Die-a-maid, or a Cleopatra, or any other heathen
goddess.   I do not think talk like that, Miss
Lucy, making love to a girl, but making game of
her ; and the girl that listens to any such nonsense,
or that hasn't the sense to see there is no sincerity
in it, is a fool, and does not deserve the real love
of an honest-hearted Irishman.   See me now,
Miss Lucy, and understand me right, when I say
there is no happiness this world could afford equal
to that which I would feel in making love to you
—that is, in telling you, that of all the women I
ever saw, I would, if I was an emperor, choose
you for my wife, beyond the rest of womankind.
And, what I mean by ' making love' is, that when
I told you so, you would believe me—feel quite
sure that I was saying nothing but the truth. And
then—believing in my truth, that you would just

think to yourself, whether or not, such love and such truth were not worthy of some return ; or whether, if a woman has made up her mind not to be a nun, there is any possible better chance of felicity in this life than in passing her days from youth to old age as the wedded wife of a man, who was sincere in all he spoke, and in earnest whatever he did. So, you see, Miss Lucy, your question is easily answered : an Irishman had much rather be engaged in making love than in fighting."

To this speech Lucy Watford attempted no reply.

The young Irishman and the young English-woman rode on in silence, for miles together, afterwards ; and one might suppose that there were parts of the journey in which the road was much rougher than others, for Lucy, either from fear, or unconsciously, clasped her arm tighter around the thick over-coat of Pat Kinchela.

Pat Kinchela seemed not to be displeased at the silence of his companion, for when they reached home at last, and he was helping her off the horse, he whispered in her ear.

" Well, Miss Lucy—have you been thinking of what I was saying to you?"

" I have Kinchela," replied Lucy, dropping the Mister.

"And what is your opinion of Ireland?" asked the cunning youth.

" I think it is the finest country in the world," answered Lucy, " and I am quite in love with it."

" And have you paid any attention to the last words we spoke on the road together, Miss Lucy?"

" Call me Lucy, not Miss Lucy," said the English maiden.

" Well?" said Kinchela.

" Very well!" said Lucy, laughing.

" Give me the hand on it," said Kinchela.

" Not yet awhile, Pat," answered the smiling Lucy, as she hurried off to assist her mistress, who was that moment alighting from the post-chaise.

" Oh!" ejaculated Kinchela as he led his horse to the stable. If that *sprissaun* had but have seen me dance the 'polthering jig,' she would have said, ' to-morrow, Pat, my darling—as soon as you like.' But no matter! For one night's talk, I have not got on so badly. Well! well! well! There may be boys who have more discourse in them than myself, and it would not be hard for them to have it: there may too be others, who may beat me out in piety, and an easy job for them; but this I say, that the like of me was never before me, and the like of me will never come after me, in dancing that one jig: and, may I never die! but I will always have a spite in my heart against the Orangemen, who prevented me from going through it with Miss Lucy looking at me. Oh! if she had but once seen *that*—it isn't 'wait awhile' she would be after saying to me, but 'take me, Pat, jewel!—take me at once, for your equal is not to be found in England, Ireland, Scotland, or the Isle of Man.' At all events one thing is certain, she said 'very well.' Now, when a pretty girl says to a young man 'very well,' they are, I think, two little words that have a great deal of meaning in them. What more could she say to me than 'very well?' A man is always well off, when 'very well' is said to him. 'Well,' says I; 'very well' says she. Why, it was coming to the very point I wanted to get her—marrying my 'well' to her 'very well.' Yes—that is it, as plain as she could speak it, 'very well' means 'talk to the priest'—'very well' means 'buy the wedding-ring,' 'very well' means 'name the wedding-day.' 'Very well' means 'I am quite agreable'—it means 'yes, for ever and a day Pat, when you are well, you shall always find your own dear Lucy to be very well.'

"But shame upon you, Pat Kinchela! to be thinking of marriage at the very time that death may be in the house, and when, at all events, your young master's life is in danger! Oh! these women! how they can soften a man's heart, and harden it at the same time! But—the creatures! —they are to be pardoned and pitied for that same. It is not their fault. They can no more prevent themselves from being bewitching, than a young colt can help being skittish, nor a snipe from flying any way but in a straight line before it, nor a sweet-briar from being full of thorns."

CHAPTER III.

BALM FOR A WOUND.

WHILST the enamoured Patrick Kinchela was giving vent to his feelings, and at the same time attending to the horses in the stable, his young master, Kirwan Williams, was being conveyed with great care and tenderness from the carriage to his own bed-room, whither he was followed by Mr. Kirwan, Miss Arnold, and Lucy.

"What say you now as to the condition of your patient, Doctor Devitt," enquired Mr. Kirwan. How has he borne the journey?"

"He is suffering a great deal of pain," replied the Doctor. "Fever is setting in much sooner than I expected. I think his worst symptoms are mainly caused by his anxiety for your safety, as well as for the young lady."

"May we not speak to him?" timidly asked Miss Arnold.

"Repose! — complete repose! — absolute silence! are, in my judgment, indispensable," replied Dr. Devitt. "If it were possible, I would not have one word spoken to him, nor let himself speak for the next twenty-four hours. But the fact is, he has taken it into his head (and was raving on the same points whilst he was in the carriage) that his uncle has been slain, and you carried away by an officer. I think then, that one of the best means that can be adopted for inducing what is so necessary to his safety—complete composure of mind—is to let you and Mr. Kirwan speak to him. That I believe, on the whole, of two evils will be the least."

"Oh! do—do, sir. Let me speak but one word to him," said Miss Arnold greatly agitated.

"As few words as possible, if you please, Miss Arnold," replied the Doctor. "All that should be done is—to set his mind at rest by seeing you and his uncle in this house—safe at home. Stand then out of his view for an instant, whilst I prepare him for the interview."

So speaking, and motioning with his hand Miss Arnold and Mr. Kirwan to stand back, the

Doctor advanced to the side of the bed, where the unhappy Kirwan Willians lay as still and motionless as if he was already a corpse.

"How do you feel now, my young patient?" asked the Doctor.

"Pain! pain! pain!" replied Kirwan Williams.

"Pain! where? In your leg?"

"There may be pain there—but either I do not care for it, or I do not feel it, on account of the still greater pain—the still more intense agony I am enduring."

"Is it pain in your head?"

"I cannot tell—perhaps there is; but it is nothing to the other awful pain I am suffering."

"Oh! Mr. Williams, you must be mistaken. The only places in which you have been wounded are in your head and leg, and it is not possible for you to have pain elsewhere."

"No, Doctor, it is you that are mistaken. There are parts of the human frame for which, perhaps, anatomists have never yet invented a scientific nomenclature—those parts by which we feel and think, and where our affections, our love, and our gratitude are enshrined. Such

parts have been lacerated to pieces, and their
fibres are tremulous with torturing agony, and I
am dying—dying I tell you, Doctor—because *in
them* I have been mortally wounded."

"What do you mean, Mr. Williams?"

"Oh! my beloved uncle! oh! poor Miss
Arnold! I saw the pistol of a ruffian aimed at
the heart of my uncle, I saw a ruffian hand laid
on Miss Arnold. The villains gave me my
death-wound whilst trying to defend those two
dear beings, and now my uncle is murdered! and
Miss Arnold has been carried away to be the
victim to some cold-blooded, heartless, miscreant."

"I told you before now, Mr. Williams, that
both your uncle and Miss Arnold were safe and
well."

"Tales to amuse the weak and failing senses
of a sick man! A pleasant story to delude me!
It is a portion of your craft, Doctor, to palm
such fables upon your patients."

"I pledge you my professional reputation as
a physician, and my honour as a gentleman, that
Miss Arnold is at this moment by your uncle's
side, that your uncle is in perfect health, and

that both are back in perfect safety at Abbey-lawn."

"Then, if that be so, Doctor, why do you not send for them? Why not let me see them? I am sure they would travel some distance if it were only to put an end to this awful pain which is torturing me to death."

"And if I do let you see them, will you promise to remain quiet?—to forbear talking—and to refrain from asking further questions about them."

"Let me see them—well and safe—safe and well—and never, never, Doctor was child more obedient to its mother than I shall be to every command you choose to impose upon me."

"Very well! It is a bargain; and I rely upon your honour to fulfil it literally. Now, look up, my young friend, and see if you can recognise where you are."

Kirwan Williams, whose eyes had been closed up to this time, as if the glare of light was an additional torment inflicted upon him, here gazed about him, and exclaimed :—

"In my own bed! in my own room! in my uncle's house! If it be true what you have been

telling me about Miss Arnold and my uncle,
then they ought to be—here!"

"And they are here," replied the Doctor.

"Here! here! you said *here!*" feebly ejaculated Kirwan Williams, as he endeavoured to sit
up in the bed.

"My brave boy! my good nephew" said
John Kirwan as he stretched over his hand to
the wounded youth.

"My heroic champion! my noble-hearted
protector! Agnes comes to thank you for pre-
serving to her what is dearer than life!" said
Miss Arnold, as she clasped the hand of Kirwan
Williams and pressed it to her lips.

"Agnes Arnold again in my uncle's house!
my uncle—alive! unhurt! Both here! Both at
home! Now—now—Doctor, do with me what
you like, I shall die happy."

As Kirwan Williams uttered these words he
fell back upon his pillow, apparently lifeless.

"Away, away; both of you, and at once,"
said Doctor Devitt, " and as you value this brave
and generous young man's life, let the whole
household be kept in a state of perfect repose.
Give positive orders that no one is to come into

this room, nor to disturb us here by any questions until the morning. Send a man, named Kinchela, to me to remain all the night. My patient referred frequently to him, Kinchela; and if he should again open his eyes (which is not probable) it would be gratifying and soothing to him to see one in whom he places confidence. Tell Kinchela he is not to speak a word. Our great restorative will be repose—absolute repose! I am so anxious on this point, that if I could, I would not let even a mouse move during the next twelve hours."

"All shall be done—all attended to as you desire," whispered Mr. Kirwan as he stepped softly—but not so softly nor so noiselessly as Agnes, or even Lucy—out of the room.

"Thomas!" said Mr. Kirwan, (as he closed the door of Kirwan Williams's bed-chamber) to one of the servants he saw standing outside, "how has your master been all the day?"

"I don't know, sir," replied the servant. "I have not seen my master since he gave me permission this morning to follow you to Turview. Don't you remember seeing me there, sir?"

"Ah—and so I did, Thomas: and I am so

used to see you about me, that it never occurred to me as strange you should be there, when if I had thought of it, I would have asked you, how you came to be away from your master, and he ill in bed."

"No more I would n't, sir, only that Master James himself desired me to follow you, if I liked, and you don't blame me for going, I hope, sir; because it was a pleasanter way of spending the day, than to be moping here, doing nothing at all, sir." :

"Quite right! Thomas, quite right. Go now up to your master, and ask him how he is; and if he is not well enough to come down stairs, say, I shall, if he wishes it, go up to him. But, harkee! Thomas, say nothing to your master of what has happened to day; because if he heard it, he might—he loves his good brother so much —insist upon coming down and seeing him— and that would be quite wrong, for the Doctor has given positive orders Master John is not to be disturbed to night. So—remember, Thomas —not one word to your master about the bad work at Turview. Bad news travels fast enough, Thomas, and the last place one should be in a hurry to carry it, is into a sick man's chamber."

" If I was to get a guinea a word for telling the news, I would not (when your honor desired me not to mention it), breathe a syllable about it."

" Thank you ! Thomas, I believe you. If all who deal in ventilating what they call ' the news,' were like you, there would be less scandal in the world, and fewer heart-breaks in families. Come, Agnes, to the supper-room. We can there hear what are the tidings about James—whether he is better, or is still suffering from his sick head-ache."

" Excuse me, Mr. Kirwan, I am wearied out," said Agnes, " with the terrible events of this day. I wish your nephew James very well, and will be greatly pleased to hear he is perfectly recovered ; but after the awful scenes at Turview, and that heart-rending spectacle which I have just now witnessed, I am sure you will pardon me for saying that all my grief, all my anxiety, and all my thoughts are absorbed in the condition of your nephew, John. I really have no space unoccupied in my head or heart to afford

room for either a thought or a feeling about anybody else. God bless you! and good night,
dear guardian!"

"Good night, and God bless you!" responded
Mr. Kirwan, as he kissed the fair forehead of his
ward. "I admire you the more for what you
have said of John. He acted as if he was one of
the old Red-Cross-Knights, and if he dies now
(which God forbid!) he will die in one of the
noblest causes that ever inspired the valour of
chevalier or gentleman—that is, in defence of
female honor and virgin beauty."

John Kirwan walked slowly up and down his
solitary supper-room, the table was laid out for a
rich repast, but the viands were untasted. And as
he walked he mused over the various circumstances of the day which had in their progress
caused him so much grief and pain.

"What am I to infer from the whole of these
affairs?" thought Mr. Kirwan, "Putting every
incident together—anonymous letters—enticing
Agnes to Ireland—the accusations against myself
—the appearance and conduct of Hepenstall and
his Orangemen—the attempt to murder John—
the laying violent hands on my ward! What

am I to conclude rom such proceedings ? Plainly
—that I have aroused against myself—the Lord
knows ! how, why, or wherefore !—some wicked
enemy—perhaps a great many of them—that
these enemies are malignant, base-hearted, and
unprincipled villains—that to injure me they will
not stop at telling any lies their own foul hearts
and base fancies may suggest to them—that they
are trying to break my heart, to rob me of my
honestly possessed fortune—and that they will
not (all other means failing them) shrink from
taking my life ! Well ! Be it so ! I am a man,
and I hope I can meet death like a man. I am
a Christian—however unworthy of the great
name—but still enough of a Christian to bear in
mind—amid all crosses and afflictions that may
befall me—those words of Thomas-a-Kempis :—

" ' Whatever pains or afflictions God shall
send you, you should still be grateful; because
whatever He permits to happen to you, He allows
it to occur for the advantage of your everlasting
salvation.'

" No," said John Kirwan, forgetting his grief
in his tenderness for the reputation of his
favourite author. " I translatethat passage very

lamely and badly.   How much more consoling
it is to one's heart to repeat the very words
which Thomas-a-Kempis used, that his holy lips
pronounced, that his inspired pen transcribed :—

"'Etiam si pænas et verbera dederit, gratum
esse debet, quia semper pro salute nostra facit,
quicquid nobis advenire permittit.'

"What care I," continued John Kirwan, his
brave old heart warming with enthusiasm as he
spoke.   "What care I what falsehoods villains
may fabricate against me, or what slanders
scoundrels may circulate respecting me?   They
are but tests for my patience—trials to help me
on my way to heaven.   Shall I then wince under
them?   No! Shall I shrink from them?   No!
Shall I deprecate them?   No—no—no, for if I
were to do so, would not Thomas-a-Kempis cry
out against me.

"'Christus pati voluit et despici; et tu audes
de aliquo conqueri?'"

The meditations of the old man were interrupted by the appearance of a servant.

"Well—Thomas—what says your master—
James?"

"That his head-ache is much better, sir; but

he is not well enough to come down stairs, **and**
he will not trouble you to go up to him, **as he**
has taken an opiate. He says too, sir, he is **sure**
he will be quite well in the morning."

"How is he looking, Thomas?"

"I did not see him, sir. He spoke to me
through the door, and said he was going to bed
for the night, and not to come near him any
more, sir."

"Very well, Thomas. Let the supper-things
be removed. I feel a choaking in my throat,
and all my vitals appear turning to gall. I
am sure, if I attempted to eat a morsel of food,
or to drink a glass of wine, they would stifle
me or turn to poison in my stomach. The
world, Thomas, the world has this day given me
a taste of its quality, and it has heart-sickened
me—filled me with bitterness. Yes—yes—the
cross is heavy and hard to bear—but I *will* bear
it though it kill me with its weight. Well for
me! well for me, if I sink under it with patience,
and so win that happiness that will endure
millions of ages after this earth has passed away
—away!—and is lost for ever in the abyss of
eternity."

Endeavouring with such thoughts as these to blunt a recollection of the past, and to steel himself against the calamities he apprehended in the future, Mr. Kirwan ascended from the supper-room to his bed-chamber.

CHAPTER IV.

THE WIDOW'S STORY.

AGNES, preceded by Lucy with lights, hastened to her own apartment. Scarcely had the door closed, and the lights placed on the chimney-piece than the practised eye of the English waiting-maid discovered that the room had been visited during their absence.

"Bless my heart and soul! what is the meaning of all this! The trunks displaced! the wooden-box moved from where I put it! and—"

"Nonsense! Lucy," said Agnes, " you forget, I desired the widow Kinchela to come here and wait for me. We have staid out so late—the sad accident kept us all so much later than we expected—I suppose she got tired waiting for me and has gone home."

"Oh! there has been some one here besides the widow Kinchela—that I am positive sure of replied Lucy. "That poor old woman could not have moved any one of those trunks, much less carried from where I left it that heavy wooden box. Why, I find it difficult to lift it up an inch from the floor. And what is this?" exclaimed Lucy. "I never saw such a thing as this! It is like a knife, and yet it is not a knife. Do Irish women carry about with them such instruments as these? What can they want it for? Cutting cheese or toasting potatoes?"

"That," answered Agnes, "that is a dagger. I have seen pictures of such things before, but never a real dagger until now."

It was the Lieutenant's dagger which he had forgotten to take with him, in the excitement of his joy, caused by the discovery of the suspicious miniature.

"By what strange accident has this come here?" said Agnes, as she took the weapon in her hand.

"The widow Kinchela," suggested Lucy.

"The widow Kinchela bring a dagger here! for what purpose?" asked Agnes.

The surmises and conversation of the two

young women were interrupted by a deep, stifled, hollow groan!

"Ah!" shrieked the panic-stricken, trembling Lucy.

"Silence! silence! girl for your life!" hoarsely whispered Agnes, as she placed one hand on the mouth of Lucy, and with the other firmly grasped the dagger. "More is at stake to night than our own existence. Recollect what the Doctor said about my protector—that there was to be complete repose maintained in the house. Courage! courage! Lucy, and silence! If there be danger to either, we have at least a weapon to defend ourselves."

The words of Agnes were interrupted by a slight rustling of the curtains.

"Oh! Miss Agnes! Miss Agnes!" piteously cried Lucy, "I shall die of the fright, if you do not let me screech, or run out of the room."

"Let us see, Lucy, first whether there is any danger," replied the courageous Agnes. "Remember I am armed with this dagger. Sit down, Lucy, sit down and—be silent!"

"Oh! dear! dear! dear me!" were words

heard by Lucy and Agnes as mumbled in a strange hollow voice.

" Who is there?" asked Agnes. " What is your name?"

" Oh! it is I myself. Don't you know my voice? Miss Agnes—sure I am your own old, poor widow Kinchela."

" And where are you?"

" Here *a-lanna!* here *a-lanna!* but not able to stir with the fright."

" The widow Kinchela!" said Lucy, jumping up nimbly—"the widow Kinchela! why she is like an echo—all voice and an invisible body!" And so saying, the lively English girl snatched up a candle and added:—" If the widow be in the room, and has not grown as small and as black as a cockchafer, I shall find her."

" Oh! I am here, darlings! wrapped up in the bed-curtains at the head of the bed next the wall," cried the widow Kinchela in a piteous voice, " and you will have to unroll me out of them like a bundle of flannel, or I shall never be able to stir alive from this spot."

" Good heavens!" cried Agnes, as assisted

by Lucy, she raised the widow Kinchela from the floor, and placed her lying on her own bed. "The poor woman is dying of terror and exhaustion! What is to be done for her?"

"*This!*" said the agile Lucy, as she unlocked her own box, and produced a flask of brandy, and a large hunch of gingerbread, "This, Miss Agnes, is the best of all restoratives. I was told that the surest cure for sea-sickness was English gingerbread and French brandy; and therefore, provided myself with both for our voyage; but I was so ill from the time I went on board until I landed, that I never thought of them. Here, 'my poor, dear old woman," said Lucy pouring more than a glass of brandy into a tumbler of water. "Here, drink this off, it will do you good."

The widow Kinchela eagerly swallowed the brandy and water. A flush spread over her withered cheeks; her power of utterance was restored, and the first use she made of it was to say in a low and trembling voice, as she clasped one of Agnes's hands in her own; "Speak low —speak if you can in whispers—take care—take care *he* does not hear you, or—you will never

leave this room with life! *He* will murder you
—aye—murder you in your sleep, if *he* knows
that you know what I know."

"Compose yourself," said Agnes, looking
down upon the terrified old woman with astonishment. "Try and sleep; Lucy and I shall watch
beside you."

"Sleep! Is it *me* sleep in this house again?
and *he* in it! Not if you gave me the king's
dominions," said the widow Kinchela still trembling with fear. "But, hush! hush! hush!
darling honey! Speak lower—lower—not above
your breath. Oh! it is necessary to tell you—
but still—still—keep it a secret; or I vow to
you *he* will murder you. The devil's hand has
written 'villain' between his two eye-brows;
and I saw the word 'murderer' there as plain as
I see you."

"What do you mean? Of whom are you
speaking? Or, rather, I ought to say, who has
frightened you?" asked Agnes.

"Oh! *he*—*he*—I haven't the strength, nor
heart, nor courage yet awhile to tell you his name.
But *he* is the greatest enemy you have in the
world, darling. Listen—listen—and I will say

to you all, all—every word. Yes, darling—if I
was to lose my life for telling—still you shall
know all.   Oh! the base villain!—to steal into
a young lady's room!—and she away from home!
—to open all her trunks!—to examine all her
clothes!—to ransack her writing desk!—to look
at her letters!   Ah! Miss Agnes, my darling,
when I saw him do that, my woman's heart could
not stand it any longer, and between grief,
shame, and horror, I groaned aloud! I did indeed,
darling—I couldn't help it; and then!—if you
were to see him, with his long knife in his hand,
—like a butcher seeking for a lamb he heard
bleating, in order that he might stab it to the
heart!—and he searching all the room round for
me; and when he couldn't find me slashing
everything before him!—I am sure he has cut
through more than twenty of your finest dresses,
so that you will never be able to wear them again.
Did you ever hear of such villainy? Oh! Miss
Lucy, when I think of all the grand clothes that
rascal's sharp knife has destroyed upon your
mistress I am ready to faint off again.   Give me
another taste of that cordial.   It is almost as
good as potteen."

Agnes and Lucy looked at each other, whilst the old woman was taking the refreshment she desired. In the faces of both were exhibited the same feelings—some terror, and a great deal of curiosity.

"Oh, Miss Agnes, my own darling!" said the old woman, in a stronger voice than she had before spoken with, "How could you be so imprudent?"

"Imprudent!" said Agnes, surprised, "in what way, my kind old nurse, have I been imprudent?"

"Oh, to have a picture of a strange, lovely young gentleman amongst your secret papers! Oh, it was very foolish; but all handsome young women are foolish. I suppose I was so once myself."

"I am not aware there was any such picture amongst my papers," replied Agnes. "So make your mind perfectly easy on that point."

"Then, what did the villain mean?" said the widow Kinchela, in her indignation, forgetting her former caution to Agnes, to speak only in whispers. "What did the base, cowardly, un-manly, skulking villain mean? I was not near enough to see what he was looking at; but I heard him boasting, and bragging, and triumphing over it, and saying, 'Now that I have this picture of a young man to produce, I will make that saucy jade '—yes, Miss Agnes, the thieving rapscallion called you, yourself, 'a jade!' and then he said he would make you 'knuckle down to him,' and that you 'shouldn't have the life of a dog with him'—and when I heard, from his own lips, how he intended to maltreat you, I again groaned aloud, and then he up with his long knife again, and stabbing right and left about him, like a raging madman, and after that I fainted away, and I don't know what else he said or did, or whether he said or did anything or nothing."

"My kind-hearted old nurse!" said Agnes, kissing her on the cheek, and doing her utmost to cheer and encourage the poor woman, "I am very—very sorry you should have endured such terrors on my account; but be comforted with the assurance—I never carried any such picture about with me."

"That is strange! very strange, indeed!" said the widow Kinchela, "for when he found that picture, he was muttering to himself that he wanted to have something to prove against you, and yet could discover nothing, though he had been whole hours searching through your papers. That picture, too, I can tell you, he has stolen from you, for I saw him putting it in his pocket, and, now I think of it, he said it was—a miniature."

"A miniature!" exclaimed Agnes, starting up and trembling.

"Yes, a miniature," added the widow, "as he described it, of a very handsome young cavalry officer."

"Gracious goodness!" cried Agnes, "you do not mean to say that miniature has been stolen from my writing-desk?"

"Indeed! and indeed! and indeed again! it is stolen," answered Mrs. Kinchela.

"Oh, shame and misery! What! the picture of my beloved——the picture presented to my mother, by my father, on their marriage-day. It is the picture of my father in his youth! but, no, no, no, it is impossible! No one could be so vile, so cruel, and so wicked as to despoil me of that picture! that—the most precious possession I have in the world! The name—the name of

the wretch who has stolen that most dear miniature from me," cried Agnes, as she clutched up
the dagger.

" Oh, whisht! whisht! whisht, my darling,
or he will kill you," cried Mrs. Kinchela, her
former fears now returning upon her.

" The name! the name of the thief, Katherine
Kinchela!" said Agnes, still more excited, " the
name, I say! if you would not drive me mad!"

" Well, then, you shall have it. Put your ear
down to me, that I may whisper it so low, it may
not reach to the door, if any body outside is listening to us. The name of the thief who stole
that miniature of your father, fancying it to be the
picture of a lover, is—James Kirwan Williams!"

Astonishment—consternation — horror—fell,
with the suddenness and weight of an avalanche,
upon all the faculties of Agnes Arnold, as she
heard this name pronounced. Her blood seemed
to flow back to her heart, and a cold trembling
seized every limb. For several minutes she
remained silent, as a sickening feeling of loathing
oppressed her, and then, with difficulty recovering
herself, she said—" You tell me, Mrs. Kinchela,
that, with your own eyes, you saw this dagger in

the hands of the man, James, in my room—that
you saw him opening my trunks—examining my
papers, and—stealing the miniature—the picture
of my father—taking it out of my desk, and
putting it in his pocket ? "

"Yes, yes ; I saw all that—exactly as you
say," repeated the widow Kinchela. "And now,
my darling, that I have told you all, let me out of
this house, for *he* is in it, and my life will not, I
know, be safe for another hour, once he knows,
or guesses that I was here to look on all his
vile doings. Let me go—let me go at once, my
darling ! oh, do—let me go home with my son,
Pat—let me go at once."

"Your son, my good nurse, is engaged, and
cannot go with you to night," replied Agnes,
" but you shall be left at home in the post-chaise.
Lucy, which is it, at the back or front of the house,
young Mr. John Kirwan's bed-room is."

" At the back," replied Lucy.

" Go then, order the post-chaise out instantly.
Let it be brought to the front of the house, with
as little noise as possible. When it is ready,
return here. You can then conduct Mrs. Kinchela
down stairs : and, Lucy—you are a clever-witted

girl—attend to what I now say—it will be well, both in going down, and bidding good-bye to Mrs. Kinchela, at the door of the post-chaise, to speak to her as if she and I had had no conversation together this evening."

In a few minutes afterwards, Lucy and Mrs. Kinchela were descending the stairs together, but the widow chanced to start a topic which caused the instructions of Agnes to be forgotten by Lucy until the last moment :—

"Were you not," asked the old woman, grateful for the English girl's French brandy, " at Turview, to-day, Miss Lucy ? "

" I was, Mrs. Kinchela."

"Did you happen to notice, amongst the other servants, a poor young boy, named Patsy Kinchela ? "

" Yes—I rather think I did, Mrs. Kinchela."

" A likely boy, Miss Lucy."

" A what, Mrs. Kinchela ? "

" A likely boy, Miss Lucy."

" Likely ! likely ! I do not understand you, Mrs. Kinchela. What do you mean by 'likely,' Mrs. Kinchela ? "

" Oh, it is good English enough, Miss Lucy,

although not in use, perhaps, in your part of the country. When we say, in Wexford, a 'likely boy,' we mean a young man sufficiently well-looking for a young girl to take a liking to."

"Ha! So, that is the meaning of 'likely,' Mrs. Kinchela."

"Yes, indeed, Miss Lucy, and giving that meaning to the word, what is your opinion of Patsy? Do you think him a likely boy?"

"I am sorry to say, Mrs. Kinchela, that I did not see as much of him, perhaps, as was desirable; for he had his back turned to me the most of the time I was sitting in his company."

"Is it Patsy's back turned to such a face as yours, Miss Lucy? Well! he has not got a bit of his mother's taste for beauty in him, if such was the way he treated you. Why then—bad manners to him!—was that his behaviour to you, and you a stranger in the country?"

"Oh, Mrs. Kinchela, do not speak that way of your son; because, so far as I am concerned, I am greatly obliged to him for his politeness. No young man, so far as it was in his power, and circumstances permitted him, could be, I think, more attentive to a young woman."

"I am delighted to hear it, my dear Miss Lucy. So, then, from what you did see of him, you think him a likely boy?"

"Yes, I do, indeed, Mrs. Kinchela—the likeliest I ever saw. Oh, but I forgot," said Lucy, as she raised her voice, so as to be heard by any one who might be listening, " Here we are at the post-chaise. My young lady desires me to say to you, that she hopes you will be able to come up and see her to-morrow. She will be sure to be at home all the day. She has some nice presents for you, which she is very anxious, at the first opportunity, to place in your hands."

Poor, innocent Lucy! In those words, thus spoken aloud, were unconsciously and unintentionally pronounced—*sentence of death upon the widow Kinchela*—to be carried into execution in the course of a few hours afterwards!

CHAPTER V

THE BAFFLED PLOTTER.

THE wicked and base man, Lieutenant Williams, upon leaving the chamber of Agnes, and bearing away the spoliated miniature, was soon joined in his own room by the Red Spy, bringing intelligence that overwhelmed him with confusion and dismay. He was doomed to learn that the plot, which he had been for months weaving, had been, by incidents alike unlooked for and unexpected, rendered completely abortive.

The position of James—a commissioned officer in an English militia regiment—had gained him easy access to the Castle ; and then, his assumed zeal for Toryism, conjoined with the fact of his establishing an Orange Lodge at Turview, won for him the favour of the Irish government, as administered through the Chief Secretary's office. It rendered the leading personages there ready to receive with implicit faith any intelligence he might choose to convey to them. They accepted, therefore, as undeniable and incontrovertible truths every misstatement he wished to invent with regard to the political conduct and principles of his uncle. The promise was then given to him, that if John Kirwan should be convicted of high treason his forfeited estates should be transferred to "the loyal nephew," by whose means the rebellious conduct of his kinsman had been first made known to the law officers of the crown.

The annals of Ireland are filled with illustrations of such compacts. Treacherous Irishmen had century after century enriched themselves by shedding the blood of their own kinsmen.

When Lieutenant Williams resolved upon securing to himself the enjoyment of his uncle's property, by the taking away his uncle's liberty and life through the instrumentality of his own false-swearing, and the perjured testimony of such witnesses as he might hire to assist him, he was perfectly conscious he undertook a task, as simple and easy in its execution, as it was base and atrocious in its design.

The State supplied him, and all villains like

him, with the most complete machinery for carrying out their conspiracies against the lives and properties of others. The State supplied able, ferocious, and unprincipled crown-prosecutors— barristers, disposed before they opened their briefs, to accept all that was set down in writing for them as gospel truths. The State also put on the bench of justice cold-blooded and pre-judiced judges—eager to side with the crown on all points, and to scout the witnesses for the defence out of court; to treat them as unworthy of credit—as if they were already convicted rebels ! And, then, the State packed juries— it produced in the jury-box persons who had been purposely selected by sheriffs, because it was well known of those individuals that they would receive with implicit faith whatever was said by attorney or solicitor-general, or any other lawyer on the crown side; and close their ears— be " deaf as adders," to every fact that might be alleged on the part of the accused.

To rob his uncle, by swearing away his life, was an undertaking particularly easy of execution at that time in Ireland. Lieutenant Williams was well aware that when he, declaring himself to be an Orangeman, was the accuser, and that his uncle, the accused, was notoriously a gentleman who had opposed the formation of Orange Lodges in his district—the moment the matter came to a public trial, every word he (the Lieutenant) might say would be believed, and every argument put forth by his uncle discredited—that consequently Crime would be rewarded with the Verdict it sought for, and Innocence punished as if it had been Guilt.

Lieutenant Williams was not only a very base but a very avaricious man, and he was also a very ambitious, and, at the same time, a very young man. The uncle he intended to spoliate and murder was the guardian of a young lady very much attached to the old man—reverencing that uncle as if he had been her own father. And this young lady, the Lieutenant knew, was very rich, and judging of her by her picture—the most cherished ornament in the drawing-room at Abbeylawn—a remarkably beautiful girl. The Lieutenant's desire therefore was not only to gain possession of his uncle's property but also to have a young lady, as rich as she was beautiful, for his wife.

Lieutenant Williams was a very shrewd young man. He saw one very great difficulty in the accomplishment of this double purpose. He was well aware that though the law-officers of the crown, a packed jury, and the patronage of the government could put his uncle to death, and transfer that uncle's property to himself, still he would be, from that time forth, a man branded with infamy—that his name (in an inferior degree), would for ever be associated with baseness and treachery during his life, as detestable to the thoughts of his fellow-countrymen as an O'Brien of Inchequin, or as a Colonel Luttrell in the days of Kings Charles and James. Few ladies, he conceived, would be disposed to mingle their gentle blood with "the mulatto traitor," and of all women, the last of her sex would be that very young lady whom he most desired to marry, on account both of her personal attractions and large fortune. He was fully certain that Agnes would always regard with horror the person who had, by perjury, brought her guardian to the scaffold.

Here then was a great difficulty to be overcome by a young gentleman who wished at the same time to marry an heiress, and to despoil

" in due course of law," and by public process in a court of justice (?) her guardian of his life and fortune—the guardian too being the uncle and benefactor of the suitor and prosecutor !

It was wonderful the vast amount of thoughtful, abstruse, and very painful meditation the Lieutenant gave to this embarrassing difficulty; and how many, how various, and contradictory were the projects he devised, conned over, and rejected before he hit upon that plan, which was already so far and so well carried out, that up to the very last moment its success seemed to be inevitable.

The Lieutenant had, as he conceived, done everything that the wit of man could suggest, or industry achieve to have his uncle arrested on the vague charge of being " engaged in treasonable practices," whilst, at the same instant, and when the Lieutenant's name was as yet unconnected with the arrest, the young lady should be carried off by Hepenstall. The uncle was to be conducted to jail by O'Brien and the dragoons. Hepenstall was to take charge of the lady. In the moment of Arrest and Abduction the doom of guardian and ward was already determined.

The uncle was never to leave his prison with life ; whilst as to Agnes she was to be conveyed by Hepenstal to a house in Dublin—a well-known house in French Street. There, the unhappy girl would be completely in the power of the Lieutenant, because in the custody of women who had been for years unsexed by their own infamy, and were as dead to all feelings of pity, as to every sense of shame.

It was truly wonderful all the toil, trouble, and personal labour the Lieutenant gave to the accomplishment of this cunningly-contrived and truly infamous plot ! How ubiquitous he became in seeing that all the instruments he invoked to his aid, were preparing for the proper performance of this task, and ready to act at the moment he required their co-operation. One week he was at his uncle's mansion—the next in Dublin —the next in York—then he was back to Turview, drinking " the Immortal Memory " with his Lodge—then hastening across the sea with " the Red Spy " to deliver an Anonymous Letter— then back again to watch the delivery of letters, to intercept them when coming from Agnes—to suppress them, or to put false seals upon them—

then to Dublin to have his uncle's letters stopped in the Post-office, by an order from the Chief Secretary, until he had perused their contents—then gambling with Hepenstall, or lending the spendthrift money when he did not choose to bestow it in gambling with him—then getting drunk with Jemmy O'Brien, and making for the night, " hail fellows well met," with Keogh, Kendrick, Mallet, and other members of Beresford's corps of Blood-hounds—then once more to Turview—and then—his incessant communications with the Castle through " the Red Spy."

The Lieutenant conceived he had done everything completely—perfectly. Like many other worldlings, who believe that man alone is all-sufficient for himself, and therefore need take no account of other influences on human affairs—the gallant Lieutenant in his extreme zeal for his personal profit, and the advancement of his selfish schemes, had *overdone one thing.* And yet it was a very simple thing! One, that he could never have supposed would have marred his fortunes in the slightest degree! He had sent " the Red Spy " *too often to the Castle.* The United Irish

Society had their well-wishers in and about the seat of government, and these were on the watch. " The Red Spy " was tracked from the Chief Secretary's office to the riding-school of Beresford's corps in Marlborough Green, then to Jemmy O'Brien's den in Kevin Street, then to Captain Hepenstall's quarters in the barracks at the Old Custom-House, and then back in hot haste to Turview. Three times in the course of a fortnight was " the Red Spy "—the seemingly half-blind, long-bearded, red-haired mendicant so tracked by the messengers of the United Irishmen from the Castle to Turview, and then— when the information reached the Directory that Hepenstall was about to leave town—William Putman M'Cabe and John Hope were despatched to Turview, for the purpose of discovering what was going on; and, as it was certain " the Government " was interested in the success of the scheme, whatever it might be—to mar it, if possible !

And so, all the astutely-concocted plans of the Lieutenant were rendered abortive ! Men, of whose names he was absolutely ignorant, had, in less than three minutes, brought to utter destruction that skilfully combined plot which it had cost him weeks to contrive, and months together to put into active operation. And all this was effected by two men who, until that day, were unconscious of his existence!

Such things happen hourly, yet there are persons living—fine reasoners! great logicians! first-rate philosophers! who see events similar to what we are describing, perpetually occurring around them, and yet cannot believe there is over each— the greatest and meanest of mankind—an all-wise, ever-watchful, and unceasingly-superintending Providence. Unbelievers have eyes, but see not; and, therefore, will not join with the Christian who beholds the hand of God in all the accidents of life—of weal or of woe; and hence meekly, with humility, and gratitude declares :—

" Sine consilio et providendia tua, et sine causa, nihil fit in terra ! "

The Lieutenant lived at a period of time which was peculiarly regarded as "the age of reason ;" for the followers of Voltaire were to be found in palaces, and " Tom Paine, the Deist," could count his disciples by tens of thousands amongst the middle and humbler classes of society. The Lieutenant was infected with "the philosophy" of the day, and conceived he was but acting in strict accordance with its principles, when for the pampering of his passions, the promotion of his ambition, and the gratification of his avarice he was plunging into the perpetration of the basest, foulest, and meanest crimes. There was no sentiment of honour to influence him, no sense of religion to control him, no feeling of humanity to check him. He was his own idol. He had persuaded himself he had no soul—and all articles of faith as to an after-life were regarded by him as little deserving of respect as the grossest fables of Pagan superstition.

Such, then, was the individual who, believing in the omnipotence of his own cunning, was now learning from the confused narrative of the Red Spy, that his uncle's liberty was as yet unassailed, and that Miss Arnold's person was still perfectly free—that, in the assault upon them, three of his instruments had been deprived of life—others wounded—the whole of his party discomfited, and his astute project shattered to pieces!

The only counterpoise to all this unwelcome

intelligence was the statement, that his half-brother, John, had been (as it was supposed by the Red Spy's informants) mortally wounded.

The only momentary feeling of pleasure the Lieutenant experienced in listening to the Red Spy's narrative was the assurance that such was the fact—and he rejoiced at it, not because he had a strong personal dislike to John, but because it was the removal from his path of one who might become an obstacle—probably a rival—by his personal appearance attracting the favourable consideration of Miss Arnold.

Beyond that single circumstance, the Lieutenant heard nothing from the spy but what was calculated to fill his heart with rage and grief.

It was such an awful disappointment! It was so unlooked-for a possibility! and it was so incomprehensible that such a result could have occurred! A mere chance collection of vulgar peasants gathered together for amusement, to defeat an officer and a troop of soldiers—compelling the latter to run away, leaving three slain men behind them.

To listen to such a narrative was to listen to an incredible story.

If such seeming impossibilities could become certainties, what use for the future contriving a plan that should be based on facts and probabilities?

The Lieutenant was lost in amazement and despair; as he sat in his own room, silent and morose, looking at, but not speaking to the Red Spy, who was engaged at a table in a corner, regaling himself with food, and drinking glass after glass of Mr. Kirwan's port wine.

The silence that prevailed for some time in the apartment was at last broken by the Lieutenant exclaiming :—

" I hear the tramp of horses' feet ! And there are two carriages. My uncle, Agnes, John, have arrived ! They are back again in this house ! Curses on them ! You have Reddy, I see, told the truth."

Chapter VI.

THE SPY AT WORK.

The Lieutenant remained for a long time silent, without again addressing another word to the Red Spy.

The kind message sent to him, through the servant Thomas, from his uncle, was responded to, briefly and gruffly.

"What is the meaning of that?" said the Lieutenant, suddenly starting up from the table at which he had been sitting, with his head leaning on his hand.

"Of what?" asked the Red Spy, as he slowly filled out a glass of wine.

"The arrival of a post-chaise at the hall-door. I hear the grating of the wheels on the gravel. It is driving up slowly. Hush! Reddy—not a word! I wish to listen," said the Lieutenant, as

F 2

he cautiously opened the window, and peered into the lawn.

The Red Spy looked up, and as he saw the Lieutenant's head was not only out of the window, but that he was leaning down outside as far as he could with safety, the determined toper swallowed off his glass, and quickly filled another.

The Red Spy looked again. He saw the Lieutenant still engaged in listening to what was passing in front of the house, and again he swallowed a glass of wine, and as rapidly replenished it.

"So, so, so!" thought the Lieutenant to himself. "It is the widow Kinchela!—sent back to the Lodge in a post-chaise! Wherefore? Is there no mystery in this? Why is her son Patrick not with her? How has she become, all of a sudden, a person of importance?

"How?

"Ha! I have it! I see it all now. Hell and furies! If my suspicions are correct—I am utterly ruined! The widow Kinchela comes in and out of this mansion when she likes, at any hour of the day, as if the house was her own. There *was* some one in the room of Agnes to-day, when I was there. It was *she*! and she saw all that I did! The waiting-maid—as I understand her words—says she has not yet seen Agnes. Oh, to know—to know if that is the truth—

The reflections of the Lieutenant suddenly ceased, and grasping the arm of Reddy, he said in a hurried tone of voice :—

"Up! up! Reddy — if ever you showed activity and cleverness exhibit them now. Hark! the post-chaise is rolling away. Hurry, hurry off after it. You can—by crossing the lawn—easily overtake it. At all events, get up with it, so as to hear what passes when it stops. It stops at the Lodge. It is conveying home an old woman —the widow Kinchela. That woman, I suspect, was playing the spy upon us both to-day. I am afraid she was in the apartment of Miss Arnold when you and I were in my uncle's study—that is the room adjoining to where we were. If she was, something will be said by her to the driver which will lead us to know how the fact is; or she will be carrying back with her some presents which Miss Arnold was sure to have left for her. I have said enough. Ascertain the truth, but do nothing that may alarm her, or she will be back again here to-night. Away!"

Ned Reddy was a wonderfully quick runner ;: for, in less than five minutes after this hurried address, he had overtaken the post-chaise which was proceeding at a gentle pace, and jumping up behind, he remained there comfortably seated, until the chaise reached within twenty yards of the Lodge, when, dropping noiselessly off, he crept through the shrubs, and was within a few feet of the cottage-door, so as to hear every word of the following conversation between the widow Kinchela, and the man who had conveyed her home.

"Well, ma'am," said the driver, as he took the old woman in his arms, and placed her on the ground—doing so as respectfully and tenderly as if she was his own mother—"I hope I did not drive too fast—that you were quite comfortable whilst I was giving you that little jaunt."

"Thank you, heartily, Tim Connolly—I was quite comfortable—only one time I got a terrible fright."

"A terrible fright! Is it in the chaise you mean to say you were frightened ?"

"Yes, indeed, Tim Connolly, it was in the coach I got a terrible fright, and I am not the better of it yet."

"Ah, then, what frightened you ?"

"Why, then, I am as sure as that I am an old woman, that I felt some one jump up behind the coach ; and, for all I know, he may be there still."

"Faix! and may be he is! and who in the world can the rapscallion be that would go and play jokes on you?" said Tim Conolly, as he walked to the back of the chaise. "Oh, Mrs. Kinchela, the back of the coach is as bare as the palm of your hand. Nobody about the house! and such trouble in it now!—would go on with any tricks at this time, at all events—and if he did, and I caught him, 'pon my sowkins!—God forgive me for swearing—but I would give him such a welting with my whip, that it would take the laugh out of him for a month of Sundays. Oh, you must be mistaken, ma'am. Being lonesome that way, in a coach, of a dark night, often makes us fancy things that never happened."

"May be so! may be so ! But I would say I was sure of it, only that I know I am not rightly myself; because, before that happened, I got such a terrible fright."

"No wonder for you. It runs in the family

to-day—for there isn't a single soul of us that hasn't got a fright."

"Ah, then, Tim Connolly, driving coaches about so much as you do, you must know a great deal of the manners of young gentlemen."

"And so I do, widow Kinchela, and I am sorry to say I know a great deal more than is good of them."

"Well, then, Tim, you can tell me whether it is the fashion for the young gentlemen of these days to carry daggers in their pockets?"

"Young gentlemen carrying daggers! Oh! no! Mrs. Kinchela, not that I heard tell of. They are bad enough without that. In fact the only people, to the best of my belief, that have daggers are thieves, spies, murderers, and informers."

"Are you sure of that, Tim?"

"Cock sure, Mrs. Kinchela. And I will tell you what is more; that though I have often heard daggers spoken of, I never saw one. Did you ever see a dagger?"

"Indeed, and indeed, and in double deed, and to my own greater grief and sorrow, I did."

"Ah! then, Mrs. Kinchela, tell us what is a dagger—what is it like?"

"Well, Tim, a dagger is like a carving-knife, with the hilt of a sword for a handle."

"Oh! murder! Mrs. Kinchela!"

"And, that is not all, Tim. The blade of the dagger is about that length—that is from the tip of my middle finger to the top of my wrist."

"Oh! murder! Mrs. Kinchela!"

"And that is not all, Tim. The breadth of the blade is more than that of a carving-knife, and yet less than that of a sword; and both sides of the blade can cut like razors, and the point of it is sharper, aye, a hundred times sharper than a needle."

"Oh! murder! murder! murder! Mrs. Kinchela. It is not fair fighting at all to use such a weapon! No christian—not to say a gentleman—would ever carry such an instrument. A decent butcher wouldn't kill pigs with it."

"True for you, Tim Conolly; but then to see such a frightful thing flashing before your eyes in the light of day! Oh! Tim Connolly! Tim Connolly! When I but think of it I get such a turning in my stomach, that I must hurry

off to bed to keep myself from fainting. Good'
night, Tim, and thank you for your kindness ;
and tell Pat to come here to me in the morning,.
as soon as he conveniently can."

"That I will, ma'am," said Tim, as he
mounted to his seat. "Good night! Mrs.
Kinchela, and don't forget me in your prayers."

"Good night! and the Lord love you!"
replied the old widow, as she closed the door.

The Red Spy crept from the midst of the
flowering shrubs that encircled the cottage, and
then stole round it, looking in at each room
to which the light, borne by the widow, was
conveyed ; and never abandoning his post, until
the light was extinguished, and the old woman's
dwelling given up to perfect solitude, darkness,
and repose.

The Red Spy then returned to his employer,
and found the disappointed plotter in the same
desponding position he had been left.

"What news?" asked the Lieutenant eagerly.
"Did you see the woman alight?   Did you hear
her speak?   What did she say?   Did you watch
her in the cottage?"

"When I go upon a gentleman's business,"

replied the Spy, " the first thing I expect him to say to me—that is, if he is a born gentleman— is—Ned Reddy, my honest man, the life must be tired out of you, and, before you say one word, just oblige me by taking two glasses of wine, and it is mighty sorry I am, it is not hot spirits I have to offer you, instead of such cold stuff as that."

" Sit down—sit down, Reddy," said the Lieutenant, " and drink as much wine as you like. In fact, do as you please, only answer my questions at once; for I am. bursting with anxiety."

" That is a reasonable discourse of yours, Master James," said the Spy. " And I am going to act upon it, so instead of taking my wine out of these stingy little glasses, that look as if they grudged a man every drop he could take out of them, I will have my wine in this tumbler; for a tumbler, Master James, is a jolly-looking fellow—a hospitable utensil—it seems to say —'take a big sup at once, my man!' 'Drink to your liking, and I defy you to swallow the contents of me at one draught.' So—here goes, Master James! Your health, Master

James, I wish you luck, Master James, bad 'cess to me, if I don't. Here again, I say is your health. Better Luck ! and more sense to you— the next time."

" Better luck and more sense to me, *the next time!* There is a hidden meaning in those words, Reddy. That I am sure of. I wish you to explain them."

" Easy for me, Master James. It would not be so easy to explain what you were doing in Miss Arnold's room to-day. What in the world put it into your head, to draw your dagger, and go flourishing it about ? "

" Flourishing my dagger about the room ! " exclaimed the Lieutenant starting up, and gazing with horror at his imperturbable companion. " And so I did ! So I did ! And that accursed old woman was there all the time. Oh ! my rank stupidity not to have discovered her, and slain her on the spot."

" And would you now really, have killed the old woman, if you had found her out ? " asked Reddy—so little apparently moved with horror at the crime involved in the question—that he appeared to be engaged in examining the colour of the wine, as he placed the tumbler between his eye and the light.

"Had she ten thousand lives I would have sacrificed her, on the instant," replied the Lieutenant stamping on the floor in his rage. "Accursed beldame! she knows our most important secrets—secrets sufficient to hang us both, Reddy. She knows we were both in my uncle's room; that we ransacked his papers. Reddy, that old woman can hang both you and me."

"No—there you are very wrong, Master James. You are running away with the story. She might hang you, I do not deny it. But what could the poor old creature say against me? She never saw me—I never went into Miss Arnold's room—you did."

"True! true! quite true—but, tell me, Reddy —did you hear her say she saw me in Miss Arnold's bed-room?"

"She said nothing of the sort," replied Reddy. "She seems to me to be a very sensible, discreet, prudent, cautious old woman; and whatever she knows about you, she has up to this time, plainly kept it to herself. I could not, but for the hint you gave me—(your suspecting there was some one

concealed in the room while you were there)—have
guessed what she meant, when she described
your dagger, which she did most accurately.

"What! describe this dagger?" said the
Lieutenant placing his hand inside his waistcoat
—"Oh! my most cruel fortune! I forgot the
dagger until this moment. I left it—I now
recollect—by the side of the wooden-box in Miss
Arnold's room. Has she got it, Reddy? Did
you see it with her?"

"She may, or she may not, for all I can tell,"
replied the Spy. "She has, I know, brought
with her some things which I could not see.
Whilst watching I observed her take some things
—whether one or two I cannot tell—and lock
them in a chest of drawers by the side of her
bed. That she was in Miss Arnold's room, and
found there what was left for her by the young
lady, I am quite certain; for I saw what that
new present was."

"What was it?" asked the Lieutenant.

"The light of her candle shone quite plainly
on it, whilst she was examining it; turning it
now this way, and then that way; now putting it
out at arms length before her, and then drawing

it close to her eyes ; and in short, going on the way, all women—be they old or young behave themselves—when anything new has been given to them that they value very much."

" What was it ? " again asked the Lieutenant.

" A bran new silver cross, with an image in bright gold upon it. I never saw in my life a nicer thing—to steal ! "

Chapter VII.

A CRIME CONTEMPLATED.

The Lieutenant sat silent and frowning for a few minutes. A new, wicked and hellish thought rose up in his mind. He hoped to find in his associate, an instrument to execute it; for suddenly rousing himself, he remarked to the Red Spy :—

"You do not seem to like that wine much?"

"Oh ! thank you, Master James. It is better than nothing."

"You said something, a short time ago, I think, about spirits. Do you prefer them to wine ? "

"Well, Master James, I am no great *conney-sure* in these things. I have the simplest taste in the world, in the way of drinking—but still I must be drinking something. If I am killed with the thirst, I drink water—but, even so I prefer butter-milk to water, and I would sooner have thick-milk than butter-milk, and cream than either. As to beer and wine, I would as soon drink one as the other—perhaps, of the two, I would sooner have a bottle of strong porter, highly up, than all the wine that ever came from France, except one sort that fizzes like bottled porter—but sooner than beer or wine, bottled or not, give me a glass of Irish whiskey—for that is what I call real drinking, and nothing else. All the rest of tippling stuff is but a bad apology, and an indifferent excuse for getting drunk."

"I am glad you mentioned it," said the Lieutenant standing up, "for I am pretty sure there is in this *gard-du-vin* either a bottle of Irish whiskey, or a bottle of French brandy. I forget which. Perhaps, both.

"Both is best," answered the spy. "I do not think, however, the brandy is equal to the whiskey, because, although it is very pleasant to taste, still if you take but one glass more than you ought, it is very apt to give you too strong an idea in the morning that you had been drink-ing the night before. Give me then whiskey: it cheers you whilst you are swallowing it down,

and when you have swallowed it, the creature
never splits your head into pieces afterwards."

"Here is whiskey—pure old Irish whiskey—
I have heard my uncle boast 'there was not a
head-ache in a hogshead of it,'" said the Lieutenant as he uncorked the bottle, and placed it
by the side of the spy.

Reddy put the mouth of the bottle to his
nose, drew in a long breath, and then exclaimed
as in a rapture of delight :—

"Sweeter than new-mown hay! mellower
with ripeness than a pear! Overflowing with
fun, jokes, pleasure and laughter! No—in this
world, there is nothing to be compared to it! If
it was with a bottle of such as this, instead of a
rosy-cheeked apple Eve had tempted Adam, no
one could have blamed—at least I never would
—the old codger for making such a fool of himself. Oh! it is a temptation, which no man in
his seven senses could resist; and this I am sure
of, Master James, you have something to say to
me, very particular—something very unpleasant,
indeed—or you would never think of sweetening
it, by such heavenly drink as this. At all events,
whatever it is—here goes !—I will secure one

glass of this cream of life, if I was never to taste another."

The Red Spy filled up his glass, and then slowly imbibing the contents, he wiped his mouth with the back of his hand, and smacking his lips, cried out :—

" There is the cordial of existence ! There is the drink that would give a man courage to do anything ! What would a fellow, with a heart in his body, care for facing a whole troop of dragoons, if he had but a bottle of that inside him ! What's danger ! what's difficulty ! what's swords, or guns, or bayonets to a brave, boun-cing, tattering young fellow who had lined his waistcoat with such furiously fine whiskey as that ! Why Master James, there is nothing you could think of that he would not be ready to do for you."

" Take another glass, Reddy."

" Why, then, it's I that will, Master James, and thank you for asking me ; for this is the stuff that is worth drinking. Oh ! then," said the spy, as he filled out a second glass of whiskey —" was not this whiskey another great invention, sir ? Next to the skeleton key, it shows beyond

all other things what the art of man can do, and
what a height his genius can rise to! Yes—
Master James—take my word for it, the two
finest of all discoveries are the skeleton key and
the whiskey bottle.   The skeleton key to help a
poor man to rich men's money, and the whiskey
bottle to console him if his skeleton key should
break in the lock.   Are you listening to me,
Master James?"

"Yes, yes."

" Why, then, the only thing that puzzles me
is, why the rich people who keep all the good
things in life to themselves do not contrive to
make whiskey so dear that a poor man could not
afford to buy a bottle of it .   It's lucky for us—
the poor people—that the rich prefer wine to
whiskey; for if it was the other way, the whiskey
would be as dear as wine is now, and the dickens
any other thing we would have for ourselves
except such tap-lap as port, sherry, burgundy,
claret, and at weddings and funerals an odd
bottle, may be, of what they call (for fun I suppose) *sham-pain*.   Oh!" exclaimed Reddy, when
he had imbibed his second glass of whiskey, " Oh!
but it's it that is the elegant drinking !   Every

drop as sweet as honey, and making your mouth
and throat to feel as if you were getting crammed
with sparkling diamonds!—so lively, so sharp,
so diverting, so pleasant! What a queer world
it is, Master James, and so full of contrarieties!
To think that on the same day, and in the same
house, such an elegant, kindly, good-hearted,
good-natured thing as this bottle of whiskey
should be standing, and not a hundred yards
away from it! should be hiding, like a rat in a
hole, a busy, meddling, skulking, spying, inform-
ing, mischief-making, tale-bearing wicked old
woman, like that one, that is now snoring in a
lone cottage, all by herself, without a single
sinner near her!—or, if she is not snoring, may
be she is dreaming of all the mischief she will be
able to do you in the morning; for the last word
she said to the man who drove her home was to
tell her son Pat to be with her as early as he
could."

"Ned Reddy ——" said the Lieutenant—
and then pausing, as if there was something he
wished to say, but found difficult to express.

"Well! Master James," said the spy looking
at him askance, whilst his upper lip slightly curled.

"Ned Reddy," said the Lieutenant pausing, and slowly dwelling on every word. "I want to speak to you."

"Go on, Master James," added the spy in a lively tone of voice.

"Ned Reddy, said the Lieutenant in a scarcely audible whisper : "I wanted to speak to you about—about that old woman."

"I guessed you did, Master James, and that is the very reason I began talking about her myself," replied the spy in a careless, off-handed manner.

"Ned Reddy," said the Lieutenant, "you are letting the bottle stand idle. Why do you not help yourself to another glass ?"

"Not now—no more thank you, Master James. You look so pale, and your hand shakes so much, and there is such a trembling in your voice, that I fancy you are going to talk of some serious business. And, if so, it is no time to be drinking whiskey, as if one was engaged in something diverting, such as a faction-fight, or a wake, a wedding, or a christening."

"You are right, Reddy. I do want to speak to you of a very serious business."

"Go on. Out with it, Master James. Don't be haggling about it, as if I was a little girl you were trying to frighten, by telling her, in a bug-a-boo voice, a story about a ghost, a giant, or a banshee."

"Very well! I will not do so. You said, you guessed that I wanted to speak to you about the old woman—the widow Kinchela. What did you guess I wanted to say to you about her?"

"I will tell you, Master James, plump and plain, at once, what I was guessing or thinking about the matter. I was guessing that what you would say to me was this—'Ah, then, Ned Reddy, would it not be a wonderfully lucky thing for me, if that old woman that was in the room with me to-day was to die suddenly in the middle of the night, so that the secret she knows about me, would die along with her; because, if she lives till the morning, it is all over with me. Miss Arnold will never look at me, and there goes her fortune and herself away from me—now, and for evermore, amen.' There, then, now, that is what I was guessing you wanted to say to me."

"Come, come, Ned Reddy, you have not said all yet," added the Lieutenant, as he looked, with blood-shot eyes, at his associate. "You surely guessed that I wanted to say more—then—that I wished the old woman was to die suddenly in the night."

"Wishes are stronger than curses," sententiously remarked the spy. "Curses merely shew a man is in a passion, and has no power to help himself—but the wish to do a thing, if accompanied by a firm will, is sure to attain its end at last."

"I have the wish in my heart, and the will in my mind," said the Lieutenant.

"Faith! and if you have, you must speak out the one as plain as the other."

"Had you not better try another glass of spirits, Reddy?"

"Well, as I think we are beginning to understand one another—I will."

"That's right, Reddy. Drink it off—and now say to me, did you not guess I wanted to say something else to you?"

"Well, truth is the finest thing in the world, I am told, Master James; and, therefore, I will speak the truth out to you."

"Go on—go on, Reddy. We are losing time."

"You may be losing time, Master James, but I am not. I am spending my evening very agreeably. I am drinking the very best of whiskey, and in company with a gentleman who treats me all as one, as if I was his friend, by playing with me the game of 'guess what my thought's like?'"

"Come, come, Ned Reddy, this is trifling with me."

"Trifling with you! eh, dad! it is no trifle though to some one the matter we are both thinking of. But now—to business, Master James, I was guessing—"

"Yes, yes, that is it," added the Lieutenant, nervously.

"I was guessing, Master James, that what you wanted to say to me was this :—'As wishing will never kill an old woman, that I wish was now laid quietly in her coffin, stone-dead, and so her tongue silenced; then, would it not, Ned Reddy, be a grand thing for me if I could find a friend, a real friend, who would stand on no trifles—who would, between this and day-light, creep into the old woman's cottage—there is neither bolt, lock, nor bar upon her door—stand over her in the bed,

and there, with a towel—wringing wet—cover
her mouth and nostrils, close, close, close, so that
a breath could neither get in or out of her for a
quarter of an hour, and so stop—from this until
the day of judgment—the life in her body.
Would he not be the good, and the true, and the
brave friend who would do this for me? And
then, would he not be a wise and a thoughtful
friend to me this night, who, when he had killed
the old woman in that way, so that it would
appear she had died suddenly in her bed, by the
will of God, and not by the hand of man—would
he not be the friend, to be loved by me for ever,
who, after so disposing of the old woman, and so
silencing her talkative tongue—would open her
drawers—the top drawer at the right-hand side
of the bed—and if he found my dagger there,
take it away with him, so that, if any body should
be so ill-natured as to guess that the old woman
had not come fairly by her end, at all events, there
would be nothing to show that I had any hand, act,
or part in her death!' There now, Master James,
that is what I guessed you wanted to say to me."

"Yes, yes, Ned Reddy, you are right, That
is what I wanted to say to you."

"Oh, but I guessed a little more. I guessed that you said that, to have the old woman put out of the way, in the manner you were describing, you would be willing to give a thousand pounds."

"A thousand pounds! oh!"

"Aye, a thousand pounds! Would you not give a thousand pounds to be sure that old woman was this minute dead in her bed, and your dagger back again in your pocket? Or, to speak plainer, would you not give a thousand pounds sooner than lose all the thousands you are sure to get with Miss Arnold as your wife?"

"True, true, Ned Reddy. I would give a thousand pounds to be sure that old woman was dead, and to have my dagger restored to me."

"And you would be quite right, Master James. It would, considering the horrid dilemma you are in, be a cheap bargain for you."

"What do you mean, Reddy?"

"Why, Master James, here have I been guessing for you, for the last half hour. Cannot you now guess for me? Turn about is fair play."

"No, I really do not know what you are driving at."

"Oh, very well, Master James. I must speak

plainer, I see. All that I have been guessing about, you perceive, turns upon one question. Where is the thousand pounds to give to the friend who would do all this for you?"

"You may be certain of that sum. There are, you know, thousands upon thousands of pounds in my uncle's study."

"I haven't a doubt of that, Master James, I am sure the money is there."

"Well?"

"Well, I am sure that whatever amount of money is hidden there, it is nothing equal to the treasures—heaps of gold, silver and diamonds, that are hidden at the bottom of the ocean, and both are in the same predicament so far as we are concerned, for neither you nor I can get at them, nor lay our hands on them. Where, then, I say, is the thousand pounds?—ready money down, without which, I can do, and will do—nothing."

"Reddy, what do you mean? Do you doubt me?"

"Indeed, I don't, Master James; for I know you right well."

"Do you suppose I would not be true to you?"

"Why, Master James, you are not true to your uncle; and how could I expect you to be true to a stranger?"

"Listen to me, Reddy, I will give you, this instant, an I. O. U. for a thousand pounds."

"I know nothing of I. O. U.s, Master James. This I am sure of, I. O. U.s are not bank-notes nor gold, and—I will have nothing else."

"Listen to me, Reddy. I will give you a promissory-note for two thousand pounds, on condition I do not pay you one thousand within a week."

"You are disposed, I see, to be very agreeable. But once more, I say, Master James, without the ready-money I will have nothing to do with the death of Mrs. Kinchela."

"Then you abandon me, Reddy! What am I to do in this business without you?"

"I will take another glass, Master James, before I say a word more to you. It is curious," observed the Spy, "but the more I drink of this whiskey the better I like it, and the greater regard I begin to feel towards you for giving it to me. And, now, let me speak plain, common-sense to you. You have not got the thousand pounds; and though I am very fond of money, and such a large sum as that would make a made-man of me, still it is the truth, and nothing but the plain truth I tell you, when I say—I am, of the two, more glad than sorry, that you have not a thousand pounds in money to put into my hands this night."

" Not sorry that I cannot give you a thousand pounds," cried the Lieutenant looking astonished at the complacent countenance, and self-satisfied demeanour of the ruffian who was sitting and drinking opposite to him.

"Why, then, no—not a bit sorry—the more I think of it, Master James. Do you know why? Because, if you had that money, I am quite sure I would take it, and just treat the old woman, as I was saying—that is smother her with a wet towel so that there would be no appearance of violence about her, and every one that looked at her corpse the next morning would fancy she had died of her own accord in her sleep. Yes, I *would* do all that for a thousand pounds, but—not a farthing less. Even, for that sum, it would be money very hard earned I can tell you. I do not think, Master James, I am a bit too tender-hearted. I need not be mealy-mouthed in talking to you, Master James, and, therefore, I say of myself to yourself that I do not know the deed of blood or violence I would not be ready and willing to commit if I was well paid for it, or that my spirit was up, and my passions roused, and the thirst for blood really awakened. But, still and all, for me to go into that poor woman's room—to her that I never spoke to in my life, that I never saw until this night—a hard-working creature all her days —one that had never done me any harm—that had never said a cross word to me—that never had an unkind thought about me—for me—a poor man to go and so murder a poor woman! Oh! by the Powers! Master James, I would not go through such a job—no—quite impossible, unless —I first had a thousand pounds in my pocket for doing it. Not that I care much for an old woman, as an old woman; because I think the creatures are as well out of the world as in it, and I don't see much use in them, while they stay with us. But still, this is a poor old woman; and because she is poor I had rather not lay my hands on her. Now, if it was, Master James, your aunt, or your

grandmother by the father's side, or Mr. Kirwan's
aunt, or Miss Arnold's mother, or any other old
grand lady that you were in as great hurry to
get rid of as you are of the widow Kinchela, why
then considering them not as old women, but as
old ladies, and 'having had the fat of the land all
their lives,' with servants to wait on them, coaches
to ride in, nothing from morning till night, but
good eating and drinking and all other sorts of
diversion—in fact, everything they could wish for
—why then, I say, I do not think it would be,
after all their pleasures and comforts in life, much
for one of them to go through, just to suffer
about four minute's choking; and so, Master
James, if that was what you wanted, I would do
it, and do it readily for a hundred pounds; aye,
or if you were badly off for money, for fifty, or,
may be, twenty pounds. But this is not the present case at all.   Old widow Kinchela is no lady
—she has had to bear with hunger, and cold, and
hard poverty; and may be a drunken husband,
and may be bad children—in short all sorts of
crosses, hardships, and misfortunes during her
young days and middle age of life—and then, at
the end of all—when she is old and feeble, and

might look for a little peace and quietness ; and when a nice, rich, young lady has taken a liking for her, and when therefore she might be sure she would never again feel the pangs of hunger—at such a time as that—for me ! beyond all others —me, that, have no grudge against her, to stifle her sleeping in her bed ! Oh ! by Gorra ! Master James, I could not do it for—less than a thousand pounds ; and, as you have not the money, I now tell you plainly and plumply, I won't do it—no —though you went down on your two bended knees, and gave me my fist full of I. O. U.s, and my hat full of promissory-notes."

"Then, what on earth am I to do ? " said the Lieutenant, completely confounded by this outburst from his associate. " Is this woman to be allowed to live—that she may in the morning be my accuser with Miss Arnold ? "

" It is a very unpleasant look out—it is like a man seeing a rock rolling down a mountain that he is sure will crush him to pieces if he remains standing where he is."

" Then what am I to do ? "

" Do it yourself."

" Do it myself ! "

"Yes—do it yourself. You are the only one in the world that has any right to wish Mrs. Kinchela dead. You are strong enough to do it. Poor old woman ! she would not be able to stir or struggle long against you, or the likes of you."

"To do such a deed—myself."

"Yes. When a man wants a thing well done, he always does it himself. If you go about it, I am sure there will be little chance of the old woman ever saying, 'good morning' to anybody in this life, after your heavy black hand is laid upon her."

"You will not, you say, do it for me ?"

"There is no use in talking any more on that point, Master James. Even if I had the thousand I had rather not do it; and now that I see you haven't the money, I tell you—and it is the truth—I could not do it. I am not likely to be afraid, Master James, without cause; but this I tell you, I saw that old woman's face when she was talking to the coachman, and this is what I think of her : if ever there was a human being that passed through life without thinking evil of another—if ever there was a woman in whose heart there never rankled for one half-minute a feeling of envy, malice, or hatred against her fellow-creatures, that old woman is the widow Kinchela I saw this night.   I felt—what I never felt before—that there I was standing looking at a poor mortal whose life was drawing to a close, and who was sure, whenever she was called away from the earth, to be an angel in heaven, that is, supposing there is such a place as heaven, and that there are beings called ' angels ' to inhabit it.   That, Master James, was the way I felt in looking at that old woman ; and if, after that, I was to murder her—for that is the right word, Master James—if I, in cold blood, and without provocation was to murder her—why, I am as sure as that this bottle is in my hand, that a quiet wink of sleep I never would have afterwards ; and that her face—the face I saw to-night— would be gazing—always gazing into my two eyes, so that I never could see anything but that same face—that holy and saintly smile ever afterwards.   So once again, Master James, and for the last time I say, I couldn't and I wouldn't murder the widow Kinchela."

"It must be done !—it must be done !" said the Lieutenant standing up.   "The old witch has

thrust herself between me and Miss Arnold. If
she lives to tell my secret, I am destroyed.
There is but one way to save myself, and that is
—to slay her! And—since it cannot be avoided
—with my own hands."

"It is a bad job—a horrid, nasty, dirty,
ugly, bloody-minded, cowardly, unmanly job,"
said the Spy as he sipped his glass, and looked
up at the Lieutenant. "I had rather it was not
done at all; but if it must be done, all I can say
is, I am rejoiced to be out of it. I will take no
act or part in it."

"What!" said the Lieutenant, "will you
not come with me, even as far as the cottage-
door?"

"Knowing—No!—not knowing; for how
can I know what is passing in your heart?—
but suspecting what would be bringing you to
the widow Kinchela's door at this hour of the
night, I will not stir one step in that direction."

"Then, if you will not come with me—tell
me what am I to do?"

"I won't do that neither. I told you before
what I would do, if I was to undertake such
a thing. Having said that, I will not say

another word, and I am beginning to think, I have said too much already."

"Very well, Ned Reddy, I must do as best I can to save myself from ruin. I will go alone."

"That is the right way to act, for then there is nobody to tell on you, but yourself. Had I any such business on hand, sooner than ask any one to come with me, I would pay them for staying away from me, and for not letting on that they ever dreamed, I had any such bad thoughts about me."

"You are, I dare say, right Reddy. One thing, however, you can do for me."

"What is it, Master James?"

"Remain in this room until I return."

"Yes, Master James, that I'll do for you. with a heart-and-a-half; for it would pain my feelings greatly to leave this bottle until I had finished it."

"Now then," said the Lieutenant, "to accomplish this desperate task. Accursed old beldame! why should she intrude herself into my affairs, and so compel me to do what is most loathsome to me?"

"That is the right word for it, Master

James. It is indeed, the loathsomest thing that
a man—a young man—a fine young man—a
gallant officer to boot—ever did !   To choke a
weak, feeble, helpless old woman in her quiet,
innocent sleep !   Oh ! of all the rascally, cowardly
deeds that ever was thought of; there is nothing
half so bad as that ! "

"Confusion !" groaned out the Lieutenant.
"Do you wish to drive me mad, Reddy ?   Is it
not bad enough to have to commit such a crime
—why speak about it ? "

"Because, Master James, *this* is the only
time to speak about it.   It is still a thing—not
done.   An hour hence—when it is done—there
would be no use in saying a word on the
subject."

"Would," said the Lieutenant, "it was then
an hour hence, and that all was over."

"Oh ! I see," said the Spy, "there is no use
in my talking any more to you.   You will do it.
That I am sure of; for I see in your flashing
eyes 'murder' printed in letters of fire.   Ah !
then, Master James, considering you never had a
hand in an affair like this before, you are going
about it in a very methodical way.   I see you

have a short jacket on you—and a pistol in one of the pockets—and there is a dark lantern— and the skeleton keys. Ah! then, Master James, but you are very cute—'a wink is as good as a nod to a blind horse'—I see—you have not forgotten the towel—and a wet towel too—wringing wet—and wrapped close up tight to keep the dampness in it. Well, to be sure, you that are so capable of revenging yourself, and know too, so well how to go about it—for you! to ask another to do the same thing for you, was the height of folly! All that now astonishes me is, that you that are so clever, should ever have thought of another to help you—and to promise him a thousand pounds for it too!—Well! well! well! we are not all in our right mind sometimes. And so you are going, Master James, without 'bidding me the time of day.' That is not mannerly; but still I have no spite against you; and, therefore, I can't help telling you there is one very material thing you have forgotten; and that, if I was in your place, I would not leave this room without doing."

"What is it?" asked the Lieutenant, in a

hoarse, harsh voice—his lips and tongue dry, and his limbs trembling.

Reddy opened the brandy bottle, and pouring out about two glasses into a tumbler, he said, as he nodded to the Lieutenant.

"If I had in my mind such thoughts as are now playing like so many demons about your head and heart this minute, I would not stir out of the spot where you are now standing, without finishing off every drop of that. Generally speaking, I prefer whiskey to brandy; but going to do something—I wont say what, as you don't like the name of it—I would not drink whiskey, because it is apt to make one feel rather good-natured. Not so brandy—that is the stuff for taking every particle of compassion out of a man. Whiskey is for open fighting—brandy for what is not fighting—but death!—grim death that never shed a tear, and whose bony ears are closed to every sound of pity—every cry for mercy. Brandy then for you, that is going abroad with the life of another in your hands. Whiskey for me that am sitting here as pleasantly and as innocently as if I was thinking of nothing but a pack of cards,

a game of 'spoil five,' or 'beggar my neigh-
bour.'"

The Lieutenant drained the tumbler of
brandy to the last drop; and then quitted the
room without saying a word, or even raising his
eyes to look at Reddy.

Chapter VIII.

WORDS AND DEEDS.

As the door closed on Lieutenant Williams, Reddy jumped up and crept over on tip-toe, and placing his ear to the key-hole, thus communed with himself:—

"I can hear him! Step—step—step—as if he was walking through eggs! but still firm as a rock is every footfall!

"He is going—going——

."Ha!—that was the hall-door shut quietly too. He is gone!"

Reddy returned to his former seat, and placing a brandy-bottle on one side of him, and the whiskey bottle on the other, he filled out a glass from each—looked at them—took a few sips from them alternately, and then glancing round the room, he rubbed his hands with great glee together.

"By my word," said the Red Spy to himself.
"By my word! *Mister!* Ned Reddy, but you
are now in style! Nothing but grandeurment
all round you, and nothing but the best wine,
and brandy, and whiskey to drink ; and lashings
and leavings of all of them !

"Well! Ned Reddy, if you were as honest
as you are poor, this is not the way you would
be in. After working hard all day, it is on a
wisp of a straw you would be sleeping to-night,
with a bad roof over your head, and a worse
supper in your stomach. That is all the rich
men—the men who own such fine houses as this,
and have such brandy, wine, and whiskey to drink
—would leave and do leave, you, and the likes
of you when—you are honest.

"But, now, Ned Reddy, the case is altered—
you are not honest—you are a dirty informer—
acting the spy for the Tories—the faction beyond
all others that are down upon the poor, and who
only treat you well, because they want to make
use of you.

"Well! Ned Reddy, 'take your toll' out
of them, as long as you can, and then, if you
have the opportunity be down upon them too, as

they are down upon you, and all of your sort.
Above all things, Ned Reddy, ' play your cards '
so as to save your own life, in the midst of the
scrimmage, and to carry off (as you may be able
to do), plunder from both sides.

"So far as you have gone, Ned Reddy, you
have had a fine life of it; but nothing equal to
this night. What grandeur! To be sitting in a
gentleman's room, drinking the gentleman's
spirits and brandy—sitting quite cosy, and comfortable, and the gentleman himself—your enter-
tainer—gone out, like a thief, to commit one of
meanest, mangiest, and cowardliest of murders
that a man could be guilty of!

"Oh the dirty poltroon! To kill a poor old
woman, and to prevent her doing what all old
women are only fit for—talking—merely telling
another woman what she saw!

"Sure! of all the unprovoked murders that
ever was committed, this will be the worst of
them! He can't—it is an impossibility—he
can't have luck nor grace after it. And after it
—I think—it will be ' the best of my play,' to
keep as far away from him as I can.

"And—by this glass of brandy!—(I may

as well drink it as I have taken my oath on it)
—I don't think I would wait for his return, only
that I have a notion in my head, if ever I am
married to the pretty little wax doll of a girl, that
he is the person beyond all others who can help
me to have her.

" He must not be far off from the cottage by
this time.   I wonder will he have the heart to
go through the frightful work he has set about.
Sure ! he might spare her life by almost frightening her to death, and then making her take
her Bible-oath she would never tell on him.   If
she so swore and so said to me, I would
believe her, and let her live ; for I never saw
such a truthful face as that Mrs. Kinchela's on
man, woman, or child.

" He is opening the door by this time, I
suppose.   Now, let me think.   Will he have
mercy on her ?

" Oh ! he has little notion what he has to go
through, if he does such a damnable deed.   First
—the work ! the sickening work in killing her !
and then—in thinking, thinking, for ever thinking of that poor, old innocent face when the death-
struggle is over !—thinking of it to night ! and

to-morrow morning! and to-morrow night! and for ever, and for ever afterwards! thinking, thinking, thinking!

"He must be in the same room with her now! What is he doing? Oh! by the Powers! I can't bear thinking of it. I must drink two glasses of brandy 'as fast as shot' after one another, to drive that thought out of my head.

"Poor, old widow Kinchela! save yourself, my poor old woman! Save yourself—you are in the hands of a—gentleman.

"Oh, these gentlemen! these gentlemen! gentlemen never commit crimes! Gentlemen never steal sheep, nor pigs, nor horses, nor forge notes, nor commit murders. Oh, not they, to be sure! They are astounded at the crimes of ragged rascals like myself. They can hardly believe their ears when the gentleman-judge tells of all the poor men's offences that are set down in the 'Calendar,' and then addresses them—the good and wealthy, the virtuous and rich—as 'gentlemen of the grand jury,' or when he tells them as 'gentlemen of the jury,' that is, the little hanging jury of twelve, that they will surely go to perdition if they do not send this hungry wretch to the gallows, for stealing ten shillings worth of mutton, or that starving thief for purloining five shillings worth of bread, or pork, or beef, from their over wealthy neighbours. And then, when a poor man is accused of murder, how these gentlemen and their ladies crowd into the court to see the culprit, without a shirt on his back, accused of having committed a deed which they are horrified but to hear of, and that, in their goodness, and politeness, and gentility, they had almost fancied was an impossibility!

"Oh, no, gentlemen never do commit murders! So rest quiet in your bed, widow Kinchela, sleep peaceably—do not mind that creeping step about your room. Do not shrink from the cold, wet cloth that touches your withered cheek—it is in the hands of a gentleman—one of the 'gentlemen of the grand jury,' and you may be sure *he* will never do you hurt or harm. He could not do it, widow Kinchela. It is quite impossible *he* could think of doing such a low, vulgar, ragged poor-man's trick; for he who is now standing by your bed-side is—an officer and a gentleman.

"Yes, yes, an officer and a gentleman left this very room, this very night, to do a deed which I

—even I—bad as I know I am—could not bear the thought of committing, and which I refused to do; although the rich man would have given me his note of hand for a fortune, if I would but say, ' I'd try and do it.'

"To murder a poor, feeble, old woman, sleeping in her bed! Was there ever a more cruel, a more foul, or a more cowardly act? And yet, a gentleman went out of this room to do it— is, may be, doing it, or has now done it; and will never think of returning back to this room, until he is quite sure he has finished it completely —that the breath is stopped—the mouth closed— the tongue silenced—the body without a spark of life in it!

"And all for what? Why does the ' gentle-man ' do this most base deed—this most unmanly and inhuman act, that makes one, even with brandy and whiskey before him, almost sick but to think of it? Why is ' the gentleman ' a midnight-assassin, and old-woman-choker? Is he in want of bread, or clothes, or firing? Has he a wife, that he loves, perishing from want? Has he little children—bits of his broken-heart —crying out to him for food? Is there to urge him on to the hellish deed any one of the motives that drive the poor man to crime, and compel him to commit it, though he loathes himself for the offence he is perpetrating? Oh! no! for here the rich 'gentleman,' has more than enough to live on—plenty to eat, plenty to drink —money in abundance to throw away on his pleasures—and yet, with all this, he leaves money, food, house and drink behind him, and he goes abroad to murder a poor old woman that never in her whole life had as much as a pound note she could call her own. What a vile ruffian then is this 'gentleman,' for he has gone out in the dark night to stifle the life out of a poor creature, old enough to be his grandmother, and wherefore? For a mere trifle—because he is afraid she will tell the truth—because she will say she saw him in a lady's room; and because, if she says so, he is afraid that in addition to his own fortune, and his uncle's fortune, he will not have the lady's fortune also!

"Nothing but killing the old woman would quiet the mind of this officer!—this rich man!— this 'gentleman!' His first thought and his last thought was—to murder her!—aye—to murder her sleeping in her own bed! The mean, sordid, money-seeking scoundrel! it never occurred to him, that with all his wealth, he could easily bribe her into silence. The idea never once entered into his selfish breast, to visit the widow's house at night—not to murder her—but to say this to her:—'Mrs, Kinchela, I know that you saw me in Miss Arnold's room to-day. The reason I was there is that I am in love with her, and want to get married to her—but she will never have me, if she knows I have been skulking, as you know I was, about her chamber. My happiness for life then depends upon you Mrs. Kinchela; upon your holding your tongue, Mrs. Kinchela; and as it does, I will reward you accordingly. Name your price Mrs. Kinchela, and I am ready to pay it. How many hundreds would you like to have, for merely ˌsaying nothing? Or if hundreds won't content you, take thousands. I will give you a farm rent free— you shall have a coach to ride in, if you like. No matter what it is Mrs. Kinchela. Tell me, what would content you, and you shall have it.'

"Oh! no!—the 'gentleman' would not say *that*—would never think of saying that—for that would cost money. [He might be some hundreds or thousands the poorer by saying so : whereas murder is cheap—it costs next to nothing—it is only to be firm—steady—to hold fast your grip for a few minutes, and then—the secret is kept, well and surely ; and the ' gentleman ' returns to his home, with blood upon his hand, guilt upon his soul, but—not a shilling out of pocket !

" The ' gentleman ' has saved his money, and *only* taken away a single life—and that merely the life of a poverty-stricken old woman ! Fine gentleman ! perfect gentleman ! A ' gentleman ' that is like all other ' gentlemen ' ; for do we not see them, every day of their lives, proving that a pound in gold, or silver, or copper, or the value of a pound in anything they can eat, drink, wear, or make use of, is more precious in their sight than the life of a poor person ? What are all their laws for ' the protection of property,' as they call it, but laws written in the blood of the poor ? Don't they erect a gallows for us everywhere ?— in their fields where their cattle feed—at their barn doors where their own corn is stored, before their shop doors, and their hall doors, and their warehouse doors ? ' Kill the poor, but save the

gentlemen's money'—that is their law—that is
their practice—and this base fellow who has gone
to strangle—not on a gibbet, but in her bed—a
poor woman, only acts in the spirit of the law he
would make if he was in Parliament, or that he
would administer if he was acting as a magistrate.
He has protected his purse, and preserved his
reputation, and all at the insignificant cost of
one wretched, old and poor woman's life!

"Aye—he *has* done it—I'll engage he has
done it, by this time.

"There! then—whatever agony was endured
—it is all over now! There is the woman dead,
and the man, who killed her, ransacking her
drawers, and searching for what he thought of
far more importance and value than her whole
existence—his dagger—for what cost him, may
be, the matter of twelve shillings and sixpence!

"See, then, what a lucky thing it is to be a
strong, lusty, muscular, rich, young 'gentleman!'
and what a doleful thing to be a weak, withered,
ailing, poor old woman! The one is alive and
hearty, and the other is stiff and dead—and there
is her reward for being all her life pious, and
pains-taking, and pains-suffering. I saw her at

her prayers to night. I would like to know what good did her prayers do her! Where was her angel-guardian when the strong hand of Master James was pressing on her throat?

"Oh, I know very well what a clergyman would say, if I was to make that remark to him. He would say: 'Ned Reddy, you are a bosthoon. The angel guardian's business is to take care of the soul; and though the rich man's hand could stop the poor woman's breath (it was God's will she should so die), yet that cruel hand could not as much as take one syllable away from her prayers this night, and it could not touch her soul with sin, nor prevent the same good, pious soul, accompanied and protected by its guardian angel, from ascending to paradise, where it will be millions of ages after this world has passed away, and millions upon millions of ages to the back of them again, whilst that rich man—her murderer—and you, Ned Reddy, his companion, and all other blood-stained thieves, like the two of you, are howling in the burning, flaming, never-ceasing fires of hell. And, remember, Ned Reddy, you that are always blathering about poor and rich, that it was not to the rich, The Saviour

of the World came upon earth, but—to preach
the gospel to the poor.'

"That is what the clergy say—Catholic and
Protestant—they all agree in that part of the
story.   But then, on the other hand, there is not
a public-house a man can go into, now-a-days,'
that he is not told about what that great demo-
cratic hero, and out-and-out republican, Tom
Paine, has been saying in regard to the Christian
religion—namely, that it is not true—that it is
all an invention, and that when we die, there is
an end of us.

"Well, if that be so, if Tom Paine is right,
it is plain that this is a very badly-managed
world—that it is a fine world for the wealthy and
the wicked, and a sorrowful one for the poor and
the pious—that it is rascals who thrive best in it,
and the virtuous and the honest that are the most
afflicted in it.   And, if such was not the case,
why, I would now be starving as a poor labourer,
instead of being, as I am, housed with a rich man,
and drinking such whiskey as is now before me.

"But then, if what the clergy says be true,
that theirs is the religion for the poor—that
heaven, with never-ending joys, awaits the honest

labourer ; there is also a great inconvenience attending their religion, for a man must make up his mind to be miserable here—that is, virtuous—enjoying no luxury, nor pleasure, nor card-playing, nor big drinking ; because, if he does, he will be miserable in hell-fire for ever after.

"Oh! by the Powers! a man does not know what to do between the two opinions. The only way then is to drive all such distracting ideas out of one's head, and to stupify his brain, if he can, with good brandy and better spirits.

"One good, however, I have gained for a few minutes, by engaging myself in those troublesome thoughts on religion. I have forgotten, for the time, the cruel work on which Master James, the rich young 'gentleman' has been engaged. If ever the bad deed was to be done, it must be all over now! and the young 'gentleman' is walking back to his mansion, as quietly and composedly, and with as little fear of any bad consequences to himself for his having murdered an old woman as if all he had been doing was killing a sparrow, or setting a dog after a rabbit !

"Oh! no!—no fear of *him*, at all events— no matter how badly, or clumsily he has finished

his work.   If he has not settled the poor corpse
right in the bed ; if he has not smoothed down
the blanket ; if he has not put her night-cap back
straight upon her head ; or if he has left any mark
at all in or about the room to shew that a murderer had been at work there—little need he
care—for no one will ever think that *his* was the
hand that committed the crime !

"Ah ! if it should come to be suspected that
the widow Kinchela was smothered in her bed !
If the first sight of the dead body shews that she
has been cruelly choked, and an alarm be on
the instant given, then, Master James, never
mind—you are safe !—you can laugh in your
sleeve at all the weeping and wailing over the
corpse—neither the law, nor the officers of the
law will ever think of molesting you !   Not so,
however, the innocent, houseless, homeless, food-
less stranger that may be found anywhere within
five miles of where the murder was committed.
If any such there be—they will of course be
arrested on—suspicion !   Rewards will be offered
to bring home guilt to the criminals.   The rewards will tempt perjured witnesses to swear
against the poor, coatless, starving wretches, who

were in the first instance arrested, because—they had no money to pay for a night's lodging! And, very probably, Master James, you as a rich man may be summoned on the Grand Jury to find 'a true bill' against them! or, you may, as a member of the Petit Jury return with your fellow jurors an 'unanimous verdict of guilty' against the innocent culprits! And, Master James, you are the very boy to do that—no one more capable of acting that part, if required—you, who have murdered an old woman in her sleep, for fear she might speak the truth about you, would think little of dooming one innocent shoeless man, aye, or ten starving men to death, to save your own neck from the gallows!

"Come home then, Master James! Come home!—when you like—and how you like, for, whoever else is to suffer, you know right well the penalties of your own misdeeds will never fall upon your own head!"

The meditations of the spy were suddenly interrupted by his hearing the report of fire arms of some description at a considerable distance from the house.

"Eh! What's that?" exclaimed the spy

starting up in a state of great alarm. " What can be the meaning of that? He took out a pistol with him. What could have induced him to fire it? Oh! Whatever it is, or whatever the reason of it may be, that shot of yours, Master James, may turn out to be for you, the worst thing ever you did in the whole course of your life. What in the world can it be for? He went out on no child's play, and should indulge in no boy's tricks. A shot!—fired at this hour in the park!—is sure to be heard all over the grounds, and, may be, will rouse up all the servants in——"

The sound of another shot rapidly discharged reached the ears of the Red Spy, and cut short his soliloquy. He started with terror, and observed:—

" That last shot was much nearer the house! —and from the sharp ring of it, I am sure, the weapon was loaded with a bullet. Oh! by Gorra! its all up! Whatever it be—this is plain—the murder will now be found out at all events! What had I best do? Run away at once, or stay here?

" Let me reflect.

" If I run away now, I will leave a lot of fine drink behind me; and, may be, only run out to

be caught in the park—that is, suppose the murder is discovered, and the alarm is given, and
then—I would be found near where the crime
was committed, and who would I have to prove
that all the time it was a doing, I was staying,
innocently, in this room?

" By stopping here, I am safe for a time.

" There is no chance, or at least, a very poor
chance of anyone coming here before morning—
and then, when it is daylight, I can walk abroad
without suspicion. Yes—I will remain.

" After all, these shots may have nothing to
do with Master James; and, therefore, I may as
well keep my promise, and wait till he returns—
that is, if he is returning; and then, if he
is caught and does not return, why then—"

Reddy stopped for a moment — listened
attentively, and then clapping his hands together,
exclaimed :—

" The hall door is opened !—he is coming
terribly quickly up the stairs ! The idiot ! Is he
not afraid he will be heard? Oh ! he is here ! "

CHAPTER IX.

THE CRIME ACCOMPLISHED.

THE Lieutenant rushed into the room, gazed wildly at Reddy for a moment, and then sud-denly turning round, he doubly locked the door, shot with a trembling hand every bolt and bar across, and then in a whispering voice that sounded like the hissing of a serpent, he said : — " Hist ! Hist ! Silence, Reddy, silence !—for your very life ! Come ! Come ! quickly aid me ! What are you staring at ? Will you help me, I say ?"

The Red Spy shrunk back with horror— almost with fear—from the man who was now speaking ; for he beheld before him a figure of terror, pain, horror, and agony, such as he had never previously looked upon. He observed, as the Lieutenant turned his back, that his jacket was torn about the left shoulder, and that there was a dark wet patch upon that spot, whilst small portions of the shirt were dyed a brightish red. The left hand too of the Lieutenant was stained, and seemed to be—at the fingers' end—dripping with blood. These circumstances, sufficient of themselves to excite alarm, were, however, forgotten for the moment, when Reddy gazed in the face of the miserable being that was now addressing him. The Lieutenant's eyes were starting from his head—his teeth were clenched—his nostrils dilated—his lips trembling—his dark skin had lost its native colour, and was now of a yellow corpse-like hue—and the awful countenance was rendered still more appalling by deep long scars on the cheeks caked with gore, and on the forehead large drops of thick blood which seemed to be slowly oozing from beneath the negro-curled hair!

"Aid you! help you, Master James!" said the Red Spy, as soon as he could recover breath to speak. " What can I do for you?"

"Help me to pile up furniture against the door, to prevent anyone breaking in, and seeing me in this plight."

" Madness! Master James, madness but to

think of it ! Do you want to bring the whole of the sleeping, unsuspecting household upon you ? They would think you were insane, if they heard you at this hour of the night pulling the furniture about the room. Is there anyone in pursuit of you ? Have you been discovered ?"

"There was one in pursuit of me ; but my pistol stopped him in his career. He fired at me, as if I was a wild beast—without any reason, without any provocation on my part, but merely because I would not stop at his bidding ; and I —in return—shot him as if he were a mad dog."

"Do you know who it was you shot ?"

"I do—thoroughly well—it was one of my uncle's servants—a varlet, named Tim Connolly. He occasioaally acts as gamekeeper ; but neither he or any one else in that capacity had a right to be in the park to-night. My uncle has strictly forbidden the carrying fire-arms there at night, as he always declared that he preferred the loss of all the birds that ever flew to the risk of one poor man's life."

"And you have shot Tim Connolly for firing at you ?"

"Yes. I never miss my mark ; and at him

I took a slow, good and sure aim. I shot him right in the heart."

" Well ! perhaps he deserved it; if not for that, at all events, for something else. There were equal terms between you. He was a man as well as you, and both were armed with deadly weapons ;—but what about the poor, helpless, weak old woman that was sleeping peaceably in her own bed ? "

"She will never speak another word in the ears of any human being. It was easier to kill the man, than put her to death, I can tell you—."

The Lieutenant ceased speaking, and dropping back into a chair, he seemed on the point of fainting as the scene he had gone through rose to his memory.

"Brandy, Reddy, brandy instantly," he said, " or I shall expire on the spot."

"Nothing like brandy," said the Spy, as he poured a large quantity of the fiery liquid into a goblet. " Nothing like brandy for nerving a man to a deed of darkness, or for numbing his conscience afterwards. It is courage, before a crime ; and it is the best chance for a sleep, when the deed is done and—irrevocable."

"Oh! Reddy! Reddy!—why did you not
go for me, or at all events give me better instructions?" said the Lieutenant in a voice hoarse and
trembling with emotion.   "Oh! the terrific
struggles of that abominable, spiteful old woman!
Thrice she got away the wet cloth from her
mouth—and once, she found so much breath, as
to tell me, that she knew I would murder her
in her bed, and—and—and that she had that
very day forewarned Miss Arnold I would do so
—and when she said that—when I saw her
thus deriding and triumphing over me, whilst
I was murdering her—I know no more than this
—I never left her—never relaxed my hold on her
until—until—until I was sure—quite sure she
was dead—even though as I was so killing her, I
felt her tear my face as with the sharp claws of
a tiger; and that I was conscious she was drag·
ging my hair from my head in handsful.   Look
at me Reddy; is it not frightful?   Am I not a
dreadful spectacle to gaze at?   And yet, you told
me, it would be easily done, and there would be
no marks of violence."

"And no more there would, if it was properly done," observed Reddy.   "But a man

cannot learn to be a soldier in a day, nor all the tricks of an accomplished assassin in a single night. Have you left any marks of what you were about, after you?"

"None that I could help—none that I could avoid—none that I know of—none that I can think of."

"What did you do, when you were sure the woman was dead?"

"I gathered up all the tufts of hair she had torn out of my head—every lock, every little hair I could see and putting them in the lamp, I burned every particle."

"Are you sure you found them all?"

"Yes—I searched narrowly and minutely. I am certain I did not leave a single hair in, or about the bed."

"That was right. What next did you do?"

"I stretched her down straight in her bed."

"Very straight?"

"Yes—very straight."

"Ah! I am afraid, too straight. But go on —what did you do next?"

"I tucked the clothes in about her."

"Tightly or loosely?"

"Neither the one, nor the other."

"That is the cleverest thing you did yet. Well; and what about her cap?"

"Her cap! What cap?"

"Her night-cap. What did you do with that? How did you leave her night-cap on her?"

"Her night-cap," said the Lieutenant with surprise. "Her night-cap! I never thought about her night-cap."

"There you were wrong; for there is nothing in this world, an old woman is so particular about as her night-cap."

"I suppose there was nothing remarkable in the appearance of it," said the Lieutenant, "or I should have noticed it; for I looked at her very attentively to see if she had the appearance of a woman sleeping in her bed, and that no one had molested her during the night."

"And did your eyes fill with tears as you looked at her?"

"Curses on the old hag! no," replied the Lieutenant. "I was delighted to think she was dead—that she could not blab on me as she had intended to do. Besides, I was enraged against

her, for what she had said about Miss Arnold,
and her lies about having already told all on me;
and then I was furious for the way she had torn
my face. Perdition! I feel her scratches still
scorching me, as if her nails had been filled with
poison."

"Oh! these gentlemen! these gentlemen!"
thought Reddy to himself. "They are a different
race from us altogether. It is well they do not
set up as rivals to the poor in the trade of life-
taking. If they did—by the Powers!—they
would beat us clear out of the market; for a
poor man cannot hold a candle to them in the
way of cruelty—they are as hard-hearted as a
paving-stone."

"What am I to do now?" asked the Lieutenant.

"Before I answer that question, Master
James, I must first know exactly what you have
done. Did you bring away the dark-lanthorn
with you?"

"I did."

"And the towel—the wet-towel, you know."

The Lieutenant slightly shuddered as he
answered, "Yes."

" And the dagger ? "

" No.   I could not find the dagger,   I
searched for it, not only in the drawer you mentioned ; but every other drawer in the room, and
I could not discover it."

" Did you search under the pillow ? "

" I did—and found there the silver cross you
described."

" Of course, you left it where you found it
Master James."

" Of course, I did."

" And the skeleton-keys—you have brought
them back with you I hope.   First, because you
ought not to have left them behind you ; and
next, because I only got a loan of them for
you."

Before the Lieutenant had time to answer
this very pertinent question, the ringing of a bell,
sharply pulled, was heard by the two confederates.

" What is that ? " asked Reddy.

" A ring at the servant's-bell.   Perhaps some
one has found the dead body of Tim Connolly,
and has come to alarm the house."

" This is no time for trusting to a ' perhaps,' "
said Reddy, " A wrong ' perhaps ' may hang the

two of us—you, as the guilty person, and me, for being in your company. I must know what it means."

"Creep then down the stairs stealthily," said the Lieutenant. "You can be back here again before any one has time to come up, if any one should intend to do so. All the servants sleep in the lower part of the house, or in the out-offices. Whilst you are listening there, I shall be on the look-out at the front of the house."

"Wrap your hand up in a towel," said Reddy, "or the print of your blood-stained fingers will be on the window-sash."

Reddy crept, as he had been directed, down the stairs and heard the following conversation :—

"Who is there?"

"'Tis I—Tim Connolly—let me in; and for the love of the Lord! let me see the doctor; or else I will bleed to death."

"Tim Connolly!—bleeding! Oh! murder! murder! Tim, but it's you that are bleeding! and how did it happen at all, at all?" said the servant as he opened the door and examined the wounded man by the light of a lamp.

"Oh! Jack Phillips, my bouchal! I am

greatly afraid, I am a dead man ; for I am almost
shot through the heart—at all events not half
a foot away from the heart, the blood is coming
so fast from me.　Run for the doctor."

"My poor Tim Connolly!　The Lord pity
you!　Sure! I daren't go for the doctor, without
the leave of the master, and I daren't waken up
the master without narrating to him the whole
why and wherefore.　So, tell me your story,
Tim, as short as you like, and I'll hurry off with
it to the master, and make him listen to every
word of it, though he was to kick me out of
doors to-morrow morning for reciting it to him."

"Oh! Jack Phillips! Jack Phillips ¡ my
bouchal, I am killed this happy, blessed and
holy night for nothing in the world but by being
too good-natured—thinking more of other's safety
than my own comfort—And if it is God's will, I
should so die—why—praise be to God!　I
could not die in a better cause."

"Ah! then Tim, I wish you would stop pray-
ing, and go on with your story.　High hanging
to them!　Whoever they were—that shot you
in the heart, my poor fellow."

"Amen!" responded the pious Tim.　"Well,

now listen to me, Jack Phillips. I gave that honest, decent woman, the widow Kinchela, Pat's mother, you know, a jaunt home in the chaise to-night; and, lo! and behold you! at the end of the journey she told me, and her darling old face as white as a sheet, with the fear, that she was sure some vagabond, unknown to me, had got up at the behind part of the chaise, and rode close home with her and myself; and then she also told me of some one frightening her with a drawn dagger; and then—as I was going home, I began thinking over her words, and then I remembered, though I did not mind it at the time, that the carriage did at one time give a little jerk just as if some one had done just as she had said; and then, I thought of all the doings at Turville to-day, and how Master John came home wounded, and then I said to myself, ' may be, the blackguard Orangemen have not done with us yet; and, may be, they are going to attack the house to night; or to kill any one they can lay their hands on, and as the widow has no one sleeping in the house with her, may be the devil would put it into their heads to burn her and the lodge together,' and so, says I to myself, ' I'll frighten nobody by telling them what I think, but quiet and easy I'll make a *century* of myself, and patrol the park from one end to the other,' and so I went out with my double-barrelled gun on my—my—my—Oh! Jack Phillips! it is all over with me!"—

Tim Connolly fell senseless in the hall bathed in his own blood.

"Oh! murder! and millia murders!" shouted Jack Phillips roaring at the top of his voice; and so as to arouse the whole household in terror and alarm.

CHAPTER X.

TIM CONNOLLY'S STORY.

THE fearful cries of the horror-stricken Jack Phillips soon gathered around the insensible and bleeding body of Tim Connolly the whole of Mr. Kirwan's domestic servants. They were speedily joined by Mr. Kirwan himself, and in a short time afterwards the English waiting-maid, despatched by her mistress to ascertain the cause of the alarm, was to be seen in the midst of the frightened females of the family.

"What is all this noise about? Why is there such a clamour in the house, when you are aware of the positive directions given to the contrary by Doctor Devitt; and when you cannot be certain but a violation of them may cause the death of my dear nephew, John?"

So spoke Mr. Kirwan hastily and angrily, as he hurried down the stairs; but when the group

of terrified servants opened before him, and he
beheld a man, apparently dead, on the marble
pavement of the hall, he rushed forward, and
looking down at the face of the prostrate figure,
exclaimed :—

"Good gracious! Tim Connolly! honest,
high-spirited, good-natured Tim Connolly dead!
or—wounded frightfully! Speak! does anyone
know anything of this lamentable occurrence?
But before another word is said, let some one go
and knock gently at my nephew John's door,
and say to Doctor Devitt to come down instantly.
It is a matter of life or death. I know it puts
my dear John's life in danger to risk a disturbance at this hour of the night; but Tim's death
is inevitable if this hemorrhage cannot be stopped.
We must risk the uncertain to avoid that which
we know to be certain. Run, I say, some one—
do not stand like frightened sheep, thus gazing
at me. Go you—Jack Phillips."

"Yes, sir, certainly," replied Jack Phillips;
"but if you send me for the doctor, there will be
no one left to tell you about this accident; for
Tim, you see, cannot speak, and I am the only
one who knows anything about it."

"And what do you know about it?" asked Mr. Kirwan impatiently.

"Why, then, next to nothing, sir," replied Jack Phillips.

"Ah! you here, Lucy!" said Mr. Kirwan, observing the maid of Agnes. "Go—good girl —you seem to have more sense than the whole of them put together. Go—you I am sure will know how to do what I wish, with the least noise. Tell Doctor Devitt to come here instantly."

"Yes, sir, I shall call Pat Kinchela first,' replied Lucy, hurrying up the stairs.

"What a sensible girl that is! She knows the way without being told, of going about such a business!" wisely remarked Mr. Kirwan. "Oh! these English! Whatever be their situation in life, they seem to devote their whole hearts and souls to the proper—in fact to the very best—manner of performing its duties. Come now, Jack Phillips, tell us about this horrid affair. How came Tim Connolly to be wounded? Was it by accident? Did he do it himself? Or was the wound inflicted on him by another hand?"

"Why, then, Mr. Kirwan," said Jack Phillips opening his eyes with astonishment, as he looked his Master in the face. "What in the world puts it into your head to ask me such a bundle of puzzling questions? Why, then, barring I was a fairy, or a witch, or was looking on all the time this affair happened, instead of being fast and sound asleep, how could I tell you in what way Tim was wounded, whether accidently or otherwise, or if it was himself that did it, or if it was another that did it for him?"

"Then, you confounded fool!" said the enraged Mr. Kirwan, "if you cannot give any information upon these points, what do you know about poor Tim's unfortunate condition? You said you were the only person who could tell me anything about it."

"Well! and I told you the truth, sir. Little as I do know, it is all that anybody knows; and if Tim should die on the spot, it is all the world can ever hear, know, or tell about it."

"Go on! go on!" said Mr. Kirwan, fast losing his temper. "There is no use in saying anything else to you, but go on! go on!"

"I am going on, sir," said the imperturbable Jack Phillips.

"Tell us what you know—all you know about Tim being wounded."

"I will, sir, tell you all I know—that is all that Tim let me know."

"Oh! then, Tim was speaking to you after being wounded."

"Tim speaking to me! Oh! yes, sir. Tim was speaking to me—and to me alone; for he had nobody else to speak to. Sure it was me that opened the door for him, sir."

"Go on! go on! what did he tell you about this horrid affair?"

"Why, then, not much, sir; and the little he said it was very hard to understand; that is if I did understand him rightly; for he was reeling about, and his tongue was thick in his head, just all as one, sir, as if he was coming home drunk from a fair, and had got a beating from some one that did not agree with him."

"Poor Tim Connolly!" sighed Mr. Kirwan, as the picture of the distressed state of his faithful servant presented itself to his imagination.

"But, go on, Jack Phillips, with your story, and tell me what he said."

"Why, then, myself cannot venture to say that I understood exactly what he said; but this was the meaning I took from his words—that some way or another an idea got into his head that as the Orangemen half-murdered Master John in Turview, and as some of them 'got their bit and their sup' for that same, and as three of them had been sent out of the world *to their own place*, that they would therefore be for taking their revenge out of you, and if not out of you, out of some of your family or followers, and that they might come to-night to set fire to the house, or burn the hay-ricks, or to tear down the widow Kinchela's lodge; and—because Mrs. Kinchela was living alone—he said he took a notion into his head that he did not like to go to sleep with; and that was that they, the Orangemen, would be for molesting the old woman in particular, because the cowardly blackguards are always for attacking those they know have no fire-arms, and are not able to fight them; and then ha   g this notion so strong upon his mind, he got his double-barrelled gun."

"Go on!" said Mr. Kirwan impatiently, as he observed that Jack Phillips had come to a full stop.

"Go on! indeed! Ah, then, Mr. Kirwan, how can you be asking a man to do impossibilities? How can I go any further, when that is all I know about the whole affair?"

"Oh! you impracticable dolt! you brainless idiot!" cried Mr. Kirwan, losing all patience. "Do you not perceive that all this nonsense you have been telling me comes to nothing?"

"Ah! then, Mr. Kirwan!" said Jack Phillips, "for a kind-hearted, good-natured man as you are, you have an uncommonly ugly collection of bad names, and ill-natured words ready stored by you, that you think nothing of throwing about you, never minding whether it is a friend or a foe you hit with them. Sure, sir, if my story comes to nothing, it is not my fault. What more could I do than tell you all I knew? You would not wish me, I am sure, to invent lies, because there was a scarcity of news."

"Indeed, I would not," replied Mr. Kirwan, somewhat pacified by the remonstrance of the indignant Phillips; "for you know well, Jack,

I am willing to forgive, aye, and to forget too, every fault of which a servant may be guilty— but one—and that is telling lies. A liar is instantly dismissed by me."

"And serve him right too, Mr. Kirwan. I wish I had more to tell you, sir; and I would too, only he hadn't time to tell it."

"Who?" asked Mr. Kirwan.

"Tim Connolly, sir—for all I have been saying to you, is, as nearly as I can recollect, what he said to me; and when he had just come to that point of the story, when he had got his double-barrelled fowling-piece on his shoulder, at that very moment, he—dropped like a cock on the floor! and said—it was all over with him! Oh! but here is the doctor, sir. God send him luck! and give him the grace to put life once more into poor Tim Connolly!"

"Amen!" ejaculated Mr. Kirwan, and all the servants joined together in response to the prayer of Jack Phillips.

"There is not the slightest fear of the man's life," said the doctor, after a few minutes examination of Tim Connolly. "He has fainted from loss of blood. I am now stopping it," he added, as he rolled a couple of bandages rapidly round the body. "Let him be removed to a bed, where I can dress his wound properly; and a few restoratives will bring him back to consciousness and the perfect use of his tongue. Here, Mr. Kirwan, be so good as to be particularly careful of that powder-flask. I have taken it out of the patient's side-coat pocket. I shall want to speak to you, Mr. Kirwan in the next room. Meanwhile, it will gratify you and all here to learn that my other patient, your nephew, is enjoying a refreshing, life-restoring slumber. His repose, I am happy to say, has not been in the slightest degree broken by this unhappy incident."

In accordance with the physician's orders, Connolly was removed to a bed-room; and when Dr. Devitt saw that all things were ready for the operation he intended to perform, he said: "I need now the assistance of no one. All, therefore, will leave the room, with the exception of Mr. Kirwan."

The servants departed, and the doctor, locking the door, addressed himself to Mr. Kirwan.

"Have you looked attentively at that powder-flask?"

"Yes, I know it well. It is an old one of my own that I gave, a couple of years since, to Connolly, when I made a trifling addition to his wages, as an assistant game-keeper."

"Do you observe the indentation that is in it near the centre—a little to the left?"

' Yes. There was no such thing on it when I gave it to Connolly."

"There never was until this night, I believe, Mr. Kirwan. My supposition, from seeing that indentation, is, that the powder-flask was struck by a bullet—whether from gun or pistol I cannot tell—that the bullet was thus turned off from the heart at which it had been aimed; that the bullet then glanced off, tearing through the flesh, and my expectation is that I shall find it lodged somewhere in the back, but in no vital part, I am certain, from the appearance of the patient." The Doctor was examining the wound whilst he was thus speaking, and running his practised fingers over the back of Connolly, when he exclaimed: "and here it is."

A sharp instrument gleamed in the light for a moment, and then Doctor Devitt observed, as he held a small bullet in his hand: "There

Mr. Kirwan, you see I was right. It is a pistol bullet. I have drawn my professional inferences from the circumstances presented to my view. You are a man of the world, now draw yours."

"Alas! you have already anticipated them," said Mr. Kirwan, as a shade of deep melancholy passed over his face. "This pistol-bullet tells its own story. Poor Connolly discovered some enemy lurking near the house; and the villain—whoever he may be—sought to deprive my faithful servant of life; and so prevent any prosecution being instituted against himself."

"That is very probable; and, therefore, I thought it best that, whatever Connolly has to say should be first heard by you, in order that you might determine whether or not he should remain silent, for the present, at least, as regards the person or persons who may be implicated in his statement."

"Thank you! thank you! Doctor Devitt. You prove yourself, in this calamitous affair, not only a good physician, but a true and prudent friend."

Tim Connolly, in half an hour afterwards, was continuing the narration of his adventures, commenced for Jack Phillips, but now with no other auditors than Mr. Kirwan and Doctor Devitt. Tim spoke in a low, languid, trembling voice, and stopped and stammered from time to time; but his spirits were revived by a shake of the hands, now and then, from his master; and his strength renewed by imbibing a strong and pleasant cordial opportunely administered by the physician.

"Out I went," said Tim, "with my fowling-piece on my shoulder — the double-barrelled fowling-piece, and as good a gun, Doctor, as ever came out of the shop of Watty Cox, one of the best cheap gun-smiths in all Dublin. Out I went with my gun on my shoulder, like any lion, and the gun well charged with swan shot, and the flints, hammered newly, and the priming properly looked to—determined if I'd meet the Orangemen in the master's park, I'd pepper them finely, but not so as to kill them; for I would be very sorry that the very worst of them would not have plenty of time left to save his soul.

"Well, thought I to myself, if the Orangemen have any notion of attacking the house, or doing any one inside the park any harm at all, they will never be able to do it, without crossing from the outside of the park somewhere, so the best thing for me to do is to go and look all over the boundaries, and see if there is any mark of any strangers having come in any where at all; because, if they did, I am too old, and too knowing at game-keeping, not to find out the track of where they got inside the bounds.

"So, on I went, all alone by myself, and passing away my time, as best I could—now singing a song, and now whistling a tune, and now, may be, saying a short prayer, looking here, and searching there—now, inside the park wall, and now outside the park, and all the while—for the matter of two hours at the least—seeing nothing at all; until at long last, when I got up on the high hill, from which you can see the big house and the little cottage—for my mind was ever and always, and in spite of me, running on Mrs. Kinchela—I turned to the big house, and the place where I knew it was, but could not see it, because it was as dark as pitch; and then I looked towards the cottage—oh, Doctor, a drop of that cordial; for the same ugly feeling is coming over me I had just then.

"Just, in the very spot where I knew the cottage was—knew it, aye, as well as if I was standing by the side of it, though I was then, I suppose, a mile and a half, or a mile and a half and a half-quarter (for I never measured the distance) away from it, I saw a light——

"Oh, murder, murder! says I to myself, there is a light in the widow Kinchela's bed-room, and at this hour too!"

"What hour was it?" asked Mr. Kirwan.

"I have no watch, your honour, and I could not tell the time exactly, but to the best of my belief between twelve and one o'clock."

"And the widow Kinchela generally goes to bed at sun-set—very seldom has a light in her house. This is most strange?" remarked Mr. Kirwan.

"Do not interrupt him, I entreat you, Mr. Kirwan," said the physician. "Let him tell his story in his own way. It is, I foresee, of the very greatest importance—that we should have the honest fellow's statement of facts, full and unbroken. Go on, Connolly. Tell us all you thought, said, and did. You are not tiring us a bit. Here, take another sup. Now then—go on."

"It puts the life in me, Doctor," said Tim. "I feel it meandering through me, and nourishing me, like honey. Well! the very idea that his honour, Mr. Kirwan, is after expressing came into my mind, and 'murder! murder,' says I, 'there is a light in the widow Kinchela's bedroom. Why, the widow Kinchela must be, at least two hours, in bed, and fast asleep. What then brings a light into her room? Not herself—and nobody else has any business there. Ah, but then,' says I, 'may be she is taken ill—and, if so, it will be no harm to call and see, and ask if any body is there, that ought not to be there; and if it is herself is there, then to ask what is the reason why she, that never lights a candle, should take it into her old head to light one to night?'

"Just as this last thought came into my head—out went the light, and—all was in darkness?

"'Whew!' says I to myself 'If that was the way with you at first, I need not be frightening the life out of myself about you for an old widow-woman as you are! I may take it easy now, for by the time I get to the cottage, may be it's fast asleep

you will be again, and it is only frightening you
I would be, if I called and asked, what ailed
you!'

     "Well! I began pondering, and deliberating,
and thinking twenty different ways at once, as to
what was best for me to do—to go or stay, or
not go at all, or go easy to the place, or run as
hard as I could pelt; when—Ah! that was the
thing that frightened me—I saw the light suddenly
again!—and then it moved about!—and then
out it went again into complete darkness! I
still watched—and there was the light again!
then, out again! then light—and then darkness,
and then —no more light —— 'Ah! then,' says
I to myself—' Is it *Willy the Wisp* the old woman
is playing with her mould-six candle——?'

     " And then, your honour, Mr. Kirwan, and
you too, Doctor dear, then the idea flashed through
my mind, as quick as the best English gunpowder
in the pan of a duelling-pistol—for it made me
feel as if drops of ice were running through my
veins. ' By Gorra!' (God pardon me for swearing) says I to myself—' that light that is going
on that way is a light in a dark-lantern, and
whoever is moving it about is, most probably,

robbing the place whilst the poor old woman is snoring like a pig in her bed.' And when that notion came into my head I put my gun on full-cock, and started off like a greyhound after a hare, determined to run every foot of the way from the top of the hill to the Lodge-gate.

" I ran, and ran, and ran ! I ran like the wind, I was in such a hurry, until at last I ran myself out of breath, and was obliged to walk to recover myself from the state I was in, so that I wasn't half as soon at the Lodge as I would have been if I had taken the thing quiet and easy ; and it was well for me I was not, because then I would have been too late to see anything; whereas, by walking slowly I saw what I am going to tell you, though it would be better for myself if I didn't; because, in that case, Doctor, you would'nt have so much trouble with me—but God is good, and knows what is best for us, and always orders things in His own wise way, for His own merciful ends.

" Well, then, whilst I was thus walking quietly towards the widow's cottage, what should I see but a young man, nearly at right-angles with me, running away from the same place I

was going to, and in a straight line to the house
here.   Mind ! Mr. Kirwan and Doctor Devitt, if
I was put upon my oath, I could not swear that
I saw the person, I am talking of, coming out of
the cottage ; but, considering the direction from
which he was coming, the frightened way in
which he was running, and the manner in which
he looked back, once or twice, at the cottage
itself, I felt morally certain at the moment, that
he had been inside of it, and had taken something out of it he had no right to.

"So sure did I feel of this, that I, without
saying the time of the day to him—'by your
leave '—or 'I beg your pardon '—or 'God save
you kindly '—or 'good night,' or 'good morning,' or any other polite salutation that you give
to an honest man you meet with on the road, I
roared at him—(quietly trying to frighten him)
—'Holloa ! you thundering, murdering, blunder-
ing, big vagabond !   Stop ! I tell you this minute.
Stop running I bid you. I know what you have been
doing inside the widow Kinchela's cottage. I saw
your dark-lantern you dark-faced, black-hearted,
ugly, contaminated, God-abandoned villain. Stop
I tell you, or by the piper that played before

Moses, I'll put the contents of my fowling-piece into you. Stop, I bid you, or it will be the worse for you !' The never a stop he would stop for me ; but quite the contrary—the more I abused him, the quicker he ran, and the harder names I called him, the greater hurry he seemed to be in to get away from me.

" ' Oh !' says I to myself, ' this will never do. That thief must have some desparate bad work on hands, or else he would at all events stop to speak to me, and ask me—how I dared to abuse him.' Then says I to myself, ' whatever comes of it, I must learn the rights of this matter, for the Lord He knows ! what robbery and villainy this chap may have been committing—and at all events, I sha'nt kill him, but stop him I must.' All this time I was running, and he was running faster than me, for as I was telling you, I had run myself out of breath before I had seen him. 'Hilloa ! now,' says I, ' my fine fellow ! if you don't stop this very minute I'll be after sending after you, something that can run a great deal faster than ever you could. That I may never touch a glass of whiskey ! but I'll riddle you with bullets, until your mother would'nt know you from a sieve,

you will be so full of holes.　There now—stop—
I tell you—stop !—for the last time I bid you
stop.　Well—now—here is for giving you your
very last chance.　If at the third time I say stop,
you don't stop, off goes the gun.　Will you once?'
says I, ' will you twice ?' says I, ' will you for
the third and last time ?' says I.

　　" He ran still, I took deliberate aim at him ;
I fired and—I hit him ! as I knew I would.　I
saw him stagger forward—shake his left hand, as
if it was there he was most sorely hurt ; but my
own idea is I hit him in the back ; for it was at
that I aimed, and purposely, not at his head, for
fear I might kill him.　But what an *omathaun* I
was !—not to aim at his legs, for then I might
have brought him to the ground, and so prevented
all that happened afterwards.

　　" As it was, however, I saw that he was not
running like lightning, as he had been before, and
that I was, at all events, able to keep up with
him again.　This gave me second-wind, and I then
ran a great deal faster than before.　I found I
was gaining on him.　I shouted out to him I was
getting nearer and nearer, and that if he did not
stop, I would fire at him again, as I told him I

had a double-barrelled gun with me—and that as
sure as he ran fifty yards farther I would blow the
brains out of him.

"And when I said these words, he stopped—
as if waiting for me to come up to him ; but
never turning his face round to me.

"I walked on as peaceable as a judge, cock-
sure he was going to surrender to me, and I
intending to take him by the nape of the neck,
and—if he was not wounded—to lay down my
gun, and give him one of the greatest thrashings
he ever got in all his life, for the trouble he had
given me. And all that I resolved on doing
before I would ever ask him who he was, or how
he came without leave or license at the dead hour
of the night, into my master's, John Kirwan's,
park.

"And now, just listen to me ; for here is the
queerest and most improbable part of my whole
story. When I was in or about six, seven, or
eight yards of the villain, he turned all of a
sudden round. I could only see him for an
instant—just as little time as you would take to
clap your two hands together—and during that
one moment—it was like a flash of lightning, for

it was as sudden, as quick, and as plain—I saw the fellow had a dark mask on him, and that mask was the mortal image of Master James— only scarified a bit, and red spots on the forehead—and what between the figure and the face; or mask, like a face—I would swear it was Master James himself, only that I now know it is impossible it could be that fine, generous-hearted young gentleman; for Master James 'makes ducks and drakes' of his money amongst all the servants. I know, I say, now, it is impossible it could have been Master James; first, because Master James is at this very hour, and has been all day in his sick-bed, and next, because Master James is the nephew of John Kirwan, and that one of the Kirwans never did a base or cowardly act in all their born days. I know then I say it was not, and could not be Master James; but so strong was the likeness; or that I, in my flurry and agitation, fancied it to be so strong, that I was on the very point of saying: 'Ah! then, Master James, sure, it is n't yourself that is there, for me to be firing at you, as if you were an owl, or a bat, or a raven.' All this, I say, passed through my mind like a flash of lightning, as I saw the dark mask turned towards me—for on the same instant—I felt myself struck !—I was sure in the heart—for the pain ran through my body, from the heart, and then—how long I was lying there, I dont know—but when I wakened up again—the villain that shot me had disappeared—and I found myself all covered over with blood, and a pain in my left side ; and so I crept up to the house, and—the doctor can tell you all the rest."

" All I can tell you is," observed Doctor Devitt, " that you have had a most providential escape. The pistol was aimed at your heart, and but for the powder-flask which turned the bullet aside, not all the medical skill in the world could have prolonged your life for two minutes. But compose yourself to sleep now, as Mr. Kirwan and I have very important subjects to discuss together."

" That I will, Doctor jewel !" said Tim Connolly, as he pulled his night cap over his eyes down to the very tip of his nose. " See that now ! The villain aimed at my heart, and only for the master's powder-flask he would have murdered me. See that now ! God is stronger than the devil, after all; and—so my mother often told me."

And with this pious thought to console him, Tim Connolly was soon seen to sink into profound repose.

Chapter XI.

BREAKING THE ICE.

As the sound, regular, and gentle breathing of
Connolly announced his enjoyment of a refreshing sleep, Doctor Devitt stepped over to the bed-
side, and feeling the brave fellow's pulse said :—
"There is one patient safe for the next six hours.
I shall now go look to the other, and if he is
making the same satisfactory progress, I shall,
late as it is, with your kind assistance, go and
search for a third."

"God bless me! a third patient!" exclaimed
Mr. Kirwan, "a third patient! Is it the man
with the black-mask that Connolly fired at in the
park?"

"Oh! no!" replied the Doctor : "I am quite
sure that person, whoever he may be, has not
remained in the park. But, to say the truth, my
good, honest, simple-hearted, unsuspecting friend,

I have some misgivings as to the state of Mrs. Kinchela's health."

"Dear me ! dear me ! good old Mrs. Kinchela! my foster-sister, and my play-fellow—careful Kitty !—my little nurse when I was a boy—taken suddenly ill ! Dear me ! my good friend I shall be as much obliged to you for a professional visit to the widow Kinchela, as if it was to myself, to my two nephews, or to Agnes Arnold. I shall order the carriage for you instantly."

"The post-chaise, if you please," said the Doctor, "and be prudent, Mr. Kirwan. Do not say a word about where I am going, for all my apprehensions may turn out to be erroneous. Besides, I wish Patrick Kinchela, during my absence, to be able to give his whole attention to Mr. John —that which it would not be in his power to do if he had the slightest suspicion on what business I was leaving the house. As Miss Arnold has been roused out of her bed, I shall ask her to wait with you in the outer room, so that if your nephew John awakes in a disturbed state of mind, the sight of you both may—in my absence—again quiet him. And now, as I think of it, I should like to have the little English girl, as my companion. I observed her with **Pat Kinchela**. She had the prudence to keep back that part of Tim Connolly's story—if she knew it—which referred to Kinchela's mother. She seems to be such a very smart, sensible, handy, shrewd, and intelligent girl, that I should like to have her with me in case I wanted any slops made for the old woman. Whisper to her to put on her bonnet and cloak and come to me—to tell her mistress where she is going, but not to speak to any other person ; you can do all this for me, my dear sir, whilst I am looking to Mr. John, and giving fresh instructions to Patrick Kinchela."

" Certainly, certainly, doctor. Everything shall be attended to as you wish. But what a sad thing to think of! Mrs. Kinchela taken suddenly ill ! And then—my poor nephews ! John badly wounded, and poor James, so ill, he is not able to leave his room! Dear me! What calamities have come upon me, all of a sudden, and all at the same time !—God's will be done ! " meekly added Mr. Kirwan as he hurried out of the room to perform the different commissions entrusted to him by the doctor.

" Heaven have pity on the poor old gentleman!" thought the doctor, as he proceeded to the room of John—his patient. " That good man is as absolutely unfitted to take care of himself in this world, as if he was an idiot! He believes in every one's professions, credits all their statements, thinks that each person who speaks to him tells the truth; and because he himself would not be guilty of a mean, a base, or a dishonourable action, he fancies all who surround him are as true, as honest, and as openhearted as himself! Poor man! poor man! the mist of misconception in which he has been living all his life is about to be dispersed, just as the world is closing in upon him. What an agony! What an agony reserved for him when he discovers all the baseness, wickedness, selfishness, and guilt covered over with the thin veil of hypocrisy, he has been clasping to his heart. Poor John Kirwan! how many days of bitter thoughts are reserved for you! how many sleepless nights in store for you! when the remembrance of past times and false men force themselves on your memory! Alas! your trials and your afflictions are alike inevitable. All that can be done for you is to break your fall gradually

—to let you down step by step, from confidence, contentedness, and tranquillity to the dire depths of grief, which the disclosure of other men's iniquities is sure to awaken in your guileless bosom. To plunge you suddenly into the pit that is thus dug beneath your feet would be on the instant to break your heart. Poor innocent, simple-minded, truthful, good-intentioned, easily-deluded John Kirwan!"

A short time only was required to have all that the doctor desired carried into effect, and as that clever and astute man was, with Lucy, quitting the house he took Mr. Kirwan aside for one moment and said to him :—

"Am I not right in supposing Mr. Kirwan that you have discountenanced the forming of either Orange Lodges or of United Irish Associations amongst your tenantry?"

"Yes—yes—doctor that is the fact, I have constantly expressed myself opposed to all sorts of political and party combinations. Nothing could possibly be more displeasing to me. Every one who knows anything at all about me is aware of that fact."

"And yet your nephew James is the Master

of an Orange Lodge and has established one at
Turview."

"Oh! doctor! doctor! That is an absolute
impossibility. James has always expressed himself, in my presence, as having the same feelings
I entertain with respect to all such factious
combinations."

"If your nephew James so expressed himself,
in your presence, he did so for the purpose of
deceiving you; for he is—as I tell you—the
master of an Orange Lodge, and that Lodge has
met more than once in the widow Moran's. These
are facts within my own knowledge. Think over
them. Talk over them, if you please with Miss
Arnold; and when I return I am sure I shall
find you a much wiser, and a far sadder man
than you are at this moment."

Chapter XII.

THE DILEMMA.

The cries of Jack Phillips, when he saw Tim Connolly fall weltering in his blood, and which had aroused the whole household from their sleep, drove the Red Spy with speedy steps back to the room of his patron.

" If ever I heard the moaning sigh of a dying man, that last sob of the intermeddling Tim Connolly was surely it," said the Spy to himself. " Ah! ha! he got more than he bargained for, when he set to firing at a young gentleman, who was merely taking a little midnight walk in his uncle's park."

" Speak! Reddy! What news? What is all that noise about?" asked the Lieutenant, as he closed and locked the door behind the Spy.

" It is all about Tim Connolly being shot in the park," coolly replied the Spy.

"Who discovered the dead body?" asked the Lieutenant.

"Faith! he discovered it himself. He was afraid nobody would find it, and so he has come home with his own body, and there it is now lying a real dead body on the marble floor of your uncle's hall, as stiff and stark as a door-nail, and no more life in it than in a red-herring," answered the Spy.

"You do not mean," observed the Lieutenant, "to say that Tim Connolly has been able to walk after being shot through the heart. That is impossible."

"I am no scholar, and I cannot say what is impossible, but this I know, that it is true—that there is Tim Connolly after being shot by you in the park, now lying dead in the hall, and yet none but his own four bones carried him from the one place to die in the other."

"I never missed my aim yet," said the Lieutenant; "and I aimed direct at his heart."

"Oh! make your mind easy on that point, Master James, you did his business effectually. You have killed him, and that is all you wanted."

"Are you sure—quite sure no one carried

him to the house ; for I say there never was such a thing heard of—as a man living after receiving the slightest wound in the heart."

" I'll tell you what I am sure of, Master James—that I heard Tim Connolly speaking as plainly as I now hear you; that I heard him beginning to try and tell his own story, when he dropped dead—stone-dead—in the hall. Don't stare at me, Master James, as if I was telling you a lie. I heard him speaking. By this hand! I did—."

" But what is this ? " said the Red Spy changing his tone and manner, and a cold perspiration bursting out in heavy beads all over his forehead.

A sudden spasm of terror seemed for a moment to shake the heavy frame of the Red Spy, and then—the bantering, cringing, and occasionally sulky mode of addressing his associate was, in an instant metamorphosed into furious rage.

" What is this ? " exclaimed the Spy, as he looked at his hand, and saw that it was red with blood.

" What is this ? How came this blood upon

my hand? What have I had to do with blood this night, that this cursed mark should come upon me?

"I have taken away no life—and yet—my hand is red with blood! And considering the damnable deeds that this night have been done, I would, if this was found upon me, be condemned as a murderer, whilst *he*, who did them, would laugh as he saw me led to execution.

"Oh! Master James! Master James! you mean, murdering, skulking, cowardly, scheming, gentleman-like villain! This is *your* work! This is one of your contrivances to bring my neck into the halter, and to keep your own clean out of it. It was for this, you sent me down the stairs—under the pretence of watching for you. Yes—you schemer and you coward—you did this in the hope some one in the house might discover me—and then, with this guilt-blotch on my hand I might preach the truth till 'Tibb's eve' —that I was here in this room, whilst you were strangling the old woman in her sleep; that I was here in this room, whilst you were shooting Tim Connolly—and nobody would listen to me, nobody would believe me—for would not the stain of blood be on me?—and that alone would do—all you wanted—turn away suspicion from yourself and give me up to the hangman.

"Oh! you villain! you traitorous villain! If I did not despise you—if I did not think it contamination even for me to have your filthy blood upon my hands, I would treat you as you treated the poor widow, and choke you where you stand. But, now that I know you—now that I see what you are, I will leave you to your fate. Your cowardice will soon betray you, and I shall yet live to see swinging from a gibbet, the murderer of Connolly, and the mean, midnight throttler of an old woman.

"Blood upon my hand! And that hand never touched anything since sunset but what was perfectly innocent—tumblers, glasses, and three bottles!

"Why, then, what the clergy say must, after all be true! There *is* an Almighty-Power called Providence; and men are as liable, to be punished for conniving or consenting to a sin, as for committing it! And cunning as we are the Eye of God is upon us, and His arm can reach us and drag us from our hiding-places, as it was now

near dragging me, when I sat so sly and con-
cealed, and as I fancied, out of harm's way here,
I knowing well what this base thief was doing,
and so far from interfering with him, or pre-
venting him, egging him on——thinking I never
could be made responsible for his actions.   And
yet, when all is over, and his crimes are completed, and he comes back to hide here, and he
sends me away, in order that I may be trapped
with the signs of his guilt upon me!   Oh! the
villain, the mean, low, ungrateful, treacherous
villain.   Yes—yes—there is a Providence over
all, and I am almost disposed to believe there is
a great deal of truth in the old proverb—' Ho-
nesty is the best policy!'

"Oh! you deceitful, plotting villain!" said the
Spy turning suddenly upon the Lieutenant, and
shaking the blood-covered hand in his face.
"Wasn't that a pretty trick to play upon me?
What made you do it, you most rascally of all
rascally gentlemen?   Was I not true as steel to
you in every way?   When did I—a poor man—
ever shew the smallest disposition to play you
false—you—you—you son of a rich man, and

you grandson of a gentleman—for them, after all, are the worst names to give you—because they signify everything that is selfish, bad, base, cruel and unnatural."

The Lieutenant, first astounded by this outburst, and then alarmed at the rage of his associate, at length perceived the cause for both, and without uttering a word, laid his right hand on the blood-moistened sleeve of his left, and then exhibited the red mark which so slight a pressure had made upon the opened palm.

"Oh! *that* was it! *that* was the way it happened! and it was not done on purpose to betray me, nor to bring me into a hobble, nor to get yourself out of one," said Reddy, his rage instantly abating. "But then, how did it occur? I never touched you since you entered the room—never went next nor nigh you. How then could I get blood upon me? Ah! now, I understand it. I remember as I was creeping down the stairs, feeling the bannisters in one place a little damp under my hand. Your left hand must have been on the same spot coming up. And that is, I see, the way the blood came upon me. It must be your blood, Master James; and considering that you are in trouble, I am sorry for beginning to say what I did. But really—if you did mean to sell me—as I thought—nay, I was sure you were trying to do—then, you must allow I did not say half enough."

"No matter! no matter! not the slightest matter what you did say," replied the Lieutenant. "The important thing to be considered is—what is to be done?"

"What is to be done?" repeated the Red Spy, completely restored to his former liveliness of manner. "Let me see! Let me see! Oh! I never can do any good in trying to think until I have taken another glass of whiskey. I am quite *disannulled*, Master James, at the idea that you were trying to 'sell the pass' upon me.

"Here! Master James, here is better luck to you the next time you try to strangle an old woman, and shoot a gamekeeper," continued the Red Spy, as he tossed off a glass of whiskey; and then sitting down in a chair and crossing his legs, and bringing the palms of his two hands together, he said in a calm and unmoved voice :—

"What *is* to be done?

"Well now, to settle that question rightly, and to answer it discreetly, we must first see clearly, what *has* been done; and then we shall be able to say why anything is to be done; and then if anything is to be done, *how* it is to be done.

"Two things, we must admit have been done and very well done. The widow Kinchela, and Tim Connolly, the only two persons on this earth who could have said anything disagreeable to your feelings, have, in a sort of promiscuous manner, got very good reasons of their own for never bothering you any more.

"Very well! That being so settled, we have to reflect why anything should be done?

"There now comes the consideration : what have you to dread? First, if you have laid out the widow Kinchela in such a way as that nobody will ever suspect anything, but that she died in her sleep, then so far as regards the widow Kinchela, I really do not see why you should do anything except go to your bed, and repose there, (if you can) as pleasantly as an infant. Then comes Tim Connolly. You have shot him, you say, through the heart. There, I think, you are mistaken; but at all events, you hit him so near the heart, that I heard the death-rattles in his throat as he fell down stone-dead on the stone-floor below stairs. Then so far as Tim Connolly is concerned, I don't think you need trouble your head about him any more. He is dead and gone, and no more is to be thought about him, but to go to sleep and have—happy dreams!

"So far, so well. But then comes what is not and what was not well done. It was not well done in you to let Mrs. Kinchela *scrawb* your face all over, and pull the woolly-hair out of your head, as if you had been fighting with a legion of cats. I declare, Master James, your cheeks look as if some one had been *carding* them, and your face is as disfigured, as if you lay down on the ground for some one to drag a harrow over your countenance. That was very, very badly done, indeed, because until those scratches get well, you cannot let a decent person look at you. I vow to you, Master James, you are so ugly now you would frighten a horse from his oats. The widow Kinchela did that for you; and now, Master James, would you let me look at your back, until I see what Tim Connolly's gun has been doing with you."

The Lieutenant silently divested himself of his coat, waistcoat, and shirt, and turned his back to Ned Reddy, who still continued sitting cross-legged on his chair.

"A little nearer, Master James, if you please," said the Red Spy, " until I get the light better and clearer on your back. Eh! then, but that Tim Connolly—rest his soul !—but it's he that was a fine shot! I declare, Master James, for about the size of a dinner-plate on your back, you look as if some one had been throwing pepper on you, and your skin is as full of little *swan-drops* as a plum-pudding is of currants ; but still no harm in life is done to you. All you have to do is to get them *dawney* bits of lead picked out of your back by a doctor, and you will be as well as ever in a week afterwards. There! Master James, I have done looking at your back, and as ugly a sight it is, as one could wish to be gazing at. By the Powers! if Mrs. Kinchela made a holy shew of your face, Tim Connolly has made as bad an example of your back.

"And there, Master James," said the Spy in an oracular tone of voice ; " there, just there,

and no where else is the great predicament you
are placed in at this minute. If you don't get
Tim Connolly's shot out of your back, they will
scald the life out of you with pain ; and, therefore, you ought to see a doctor at once ; but then,
how can you see a doctor, or go out to look for
one, when ' all the dogs in the town ' would be
running after you, if they got but a glimpse of
your visage. Your back forces you to go out,
and your face compels you to stay at home.
That is the quandary you are in, and how you are
to get over it is what I cannot see all at once.
What do you say yourself, Master James ? "

" I do not know what to say, Reddy," replied
the Lieutenant. " That cursed old woman's
talons have deranged all my plans. It is absolutely necessary for me to see both Miss Arnold
and my uncle in the morning."

" Faith ! so you can ; and frighten the life out
of the two of them," answered Reddy, " which I
suppose forms no part of your plans. Meanwhile,
Master James, if I was you, I would put on a
clean shirt, a new waistcoat, and an unbroken
coat for there is no more blood coming from
you."

"I would not mind the shot in my back, if my face was well," said the Lieutenant.

"So you say now, Master James, because the shots have not begun yet to pain you. But let them stay where they are twenty-four hours longer, and you might as well tell me, you would not mind having a hundred sparks of fire burning in your back, as not mind them. The pain of the *scrawbing* will soon be at an end; but not so the bits of lead when they begin festering in your flesh. You could never stand it, Master James, barring you were a salamander, and would sooner be swallowing burning coals than peeling potatoes."

"I could bear it, Reddy—I tell you, I *would* bear it—anything sooner than the thought that my brother John, who has been wounded in defending Agnes, and therefore cannot be regarded by her but with favour, should have the opportunity of being in her society—of ingratiating herself with her—probably of winning her love—whilst I—who might mar their intercourse, or sow dissension between them, or render myself more agreeable than him—am compelled by this accursed accident to be away from her."

"It is very inconvenient, no doubt, Master James; but 'there is no help for spilt milk.' Just look at yourself in the glass, and see whether you would not do yourself more harm than good by letting Miss Arnold see that shew of a countenance you have. I protest I never saw an ugly knocker on a hall-door half as ugly, or a quarter as frightful as you are this very minute."

"Then what am I to do, Reddy?"

"What are you to do? It is, to be sure, a very puzzling question. Can't you think of anything yourself, Master James? You ought to be good at inventing a lie by this time, for you have been a long time practising that same."

The Lieutenant looked dolefully at Reddy; and Reddy shook his head in despair, as he returned the sad glance of the Lieutenant.

"There is nothing for sharpening a man's wits equal to a good strong glass of old, genuine, pure, malt-whiskey," sagely observed Reddy. "It is like a well oiled strop for a blunt razor, like a spur for a lazy horse, like a stick for a sulky ass, like a goad for a dunderheaded bull. And, therefore, I will take one more—just one more—only one more glass; for I begin to feel, as if I had gone to the very verge of my stint, when I mean to keep sober. But one, single solitary glass more, and then we shall see what will come of it."

The Spy's glass was again filled, and he was on the point of raising it to his lips, when he suddenly cried out :—

" What a wonderful thing is that whiskey! The very sight of the beautiful beads, that sparkle and cluster around the rim of the glass, as if impatient you should sip them before they burst, has given me an idea of what is the only possible course for you to take, considering the dilemma you are in, first with your face, and then with your back, Master James."

" What is it ?" asked the Lieutenant.

" First of all—go to bed !" said the Spy.

" Go to bed! " replied the astonished Lieutenant.

" Well then, lie down on the bed, and sleep —if you can—until morning," said the Spy very gravely. " Then when the morning is well up —that is, say about seven o'clock, when you are sure the servants are stirring about, ring the bell. Of course, your man, Thomas, will come to the door—and when he does, do you tell him, that you find you have got the small-pox terribly in your face, and neither for him, nor any other of the servants to come next or nigh you, for you might give them the infection ; and then tell him to get in a minute the gig your uncle uses when he drives about by himself in the rain, and that when it is ready, to come up and tell you; and not to let your uncle know you are going away, for fear he might see, and be infected by you ; and then say you will take the key of your room in your pocket, and no one is, for fear of catching the disease, to go into it, until you come back and have it fumigated. And tell him, above all things, that no one is to go within a hundred yards of you, or to look at you, or to speak to you, for fear they might catch the horrid sickness that is on you. There, now, is a brave idea for you! Master James, and I owe it all to this untasted glass of whiskey. The least I can, in gratitude do, is to drink it ˙off˙: and—now that it is down, it is the last I will take to-night; for I feel positive certain I have had enough, and just one more glass than what ought to be enough for me."

" It is a capital idea," said the Lieutenant,
" and I shall act upon it. But what do you
mean to do ?"

" Oh ! I will be off with myself, about an
hour before you call your servant-man. Meanwhile, I shall lie down on the carpet here, and
sleep as comfortably as if I was in a down
bed. It is not likely I shall over-sleep myself;
but, in case I should, you can call me, Master
James. I depend upon your not sleeping; for
you have four new things—you had not last
night—to keep you awake : first, the scratches
on your visage; second, the shots in your
shoulder; third, the wet towel of Mrs. Kinchela;
and fourth, the pistol-bullet in Tim Connolly's
carcase."

Five minutes after he had been speaking to
the Lieutenant, the Red Spy was fast asleep.

Chapter XIII.

THE MURDERER'S FIRST NIGHT WATCH.

The murderer was alone, keeping his first night watch!

The terrific, sickening struggles of the past few hours came unbidden and unwelcome in awful review before him.

The Lieutenant's conscience had long since been seared, and all emotions of pity, for months previously, stifled in his heart; for he had con·templated without a single compassionate pang, the inevitable consequences of the course he was pursuing. He had pictured to himself, his innocent uncle, his generous benefactor, pinioned as a prisoner, and led to execution! He had familiarised his thoughts to all the minutia of the punishments inflicted upon a person convicted of treason. He knew, that in the barbarous time in which he lived, the wretches to whom were confided the execution of the law, often indulged their malice by aggravating the bitterness of death—insulting the prisoner—maltreating him —where they dared or could do so, inflicting preliminary torture upon him—in most cases purposely prolonging the last agonies of expiring nature—and then, when all was over—decapitating the dead body—mocking " the head of the traitor "—treating the mangled remains with every indignity their hellish ingenuity could suggest! The Lieutenant knew that he exposed by his own false information, sustained by the perjury of others, his pure, confiding, gentle, simple-hearted uncle to all these horrors,—con · signing him—a gentleman—to the hand of ruffians: beholding him—who had never looked nor spoken unkindly to others — derided by miscreants! And, finally, fancying—and that too James could do unmoved—that he saw his uncle's grey and venerable hairs, held in the blood-stained hands of the common hangman!

The Lieutenant had thought of all this ; and

yet contemplated every part of the projected tragedy in an unrelenting spirit; because he thus only—and by no other means—could become possessor of his uncle's fortune. He, who had so hardened his heart, felt then neither remorse nor pity, when his mind revolved upon the various circumstances of the deaths of his two victims. Still, he could not refrain from experiencing a thrill of horror, of loathing, and of disgust against himself—as a man—when he pondered over the mortal conflict in which he had been engaged in the bed-room of the widow Kinchela. That was a scene, the details of which he had never anticipated, and the consequences of which he never could have foreseen. Even whilst his excoriated face and torn forehead burned as if they were streaked with flaming fire, his felon limbs trembled with a freezing chill of fear, as that awful battle made by the old woman against her base murderer was remembered, or rather contemplated, looked at, endured, as if it was even then going on, still continuing, and was never—never to cease between her and him!

It was in vain he tried to think of other things. It was in vain he sought to conjure out of his imagination the pictured shadows of events yet to come—to fancy himself as he would be —perhaps a month hence—the inheritor, the sole possessor of those estates, of which his uncle was then the owner—himself courted by the rich, and crowds of tenants and dependents bowing down before him. It was in vain he endeavoured to occupy his mind with calculations of his yearly expenditure—the cost of carriages—the maintenance of his houses in town and country —the purchase of a palatial residence in Stephens Green—of the magnificent reception that would be given to him at the Castle by the Lord Lieutenant—of how he would deport himself if a baronetcy were offered to him; and how much larger would be his outlay annually if he accepted of such a title. And then—he tried to weary out his spirit in sums of arithmetic, as to what might be the amount of his fortune some twenty years hence, if he commenced the day he was united in marriage with Agnes Arnold to live like a miser on five hundred a year, and save all the rest—putting by all her wealth and his own —lending money on mortgages—what it would all be with compound interest. Thus so tried with such calculations as to the future, to forget the present; and yet in the midst of those multitudinous projects, disturbing all those fancies, and breaking to pieces all those visions, there came thrusting itself in upon him, and in his own despite too, the terrific death-struggle—and *there* was the old woman still disfiguring his face with her talons of fire, and her last words ringing in his ears, and her last gurgling moans sobbing by his side; even while she is, as it were, ever creeping stealthily around his pillow, and then pouncing upon his chest, and then clinging to his wind-pipe, and then—stifling him as he had stifled her!

The murderer was alone, keeping his first night-watch.

He took no note of time, for this passing moment was like to that which had preceded it —as this hour was the same as the last—and the next hour would be but a repetition of what had gone before, and each was, in itself, the second as the minute, and the minute as the hour, dark and dread, an eternity of horror and agony—so prolonged and yet so much the same, that in the unvarying course of torture, there was nothing whereby to measure its advancement or its retardation.

The murderer was alone, keeping his first night-watch.

He could not tell how long he had been lying upon his bed—a bed of suffering—un-visited amid all its agonies, with one particle of remorse, when he was startled by hearing the sound of carriage wheels. He had only time to get to the window, to open it slowly (for fear of being heard), and to look out—but only to see the vehicle driving away from the house—and so he was left in complete ignorance either as to who was in it, or what might be its destination.

" What can be the meaning of this?" said the Lieutenant, as he looked out of the window. "The carriage is driven away at a very rapid pace—as if it was conveying some person who intended to travel a long distance. Can it have

any relation or connection with my affairs? What
on earth could it have to do with me? No one,
but those who are dead, and the Red Spy lying
there, could be conscious of the events of the
night. But, why then, is the carriage sent away
in such speed? Oh! my brother John! I forgot
him. He is the cause. That is it. Perhaps,
additional medical aid is required; or, perhaps,
and I hope this may be the case, John may be
dying, and, no doubt, he, the fool! has desired
to see a clergyman. Aye! aye! I have guessed
right. That is it—that must be it. Good! dear!
pious! John could never think of dying unless
he had some gospel-monger to help him on
the road to oblivion. That is it. That is it.
They have sent for a clergyman to go through
the mummery of prayers with John; and I
will not disturb the Red Spy's sleep to tell
him so."

Again the Lieutenant flung himself upon the
bed, and again the fearful scenes of the past
night gathered around his pillow, and again the
widow Kinchela sat, in spirit, by his bedside, and
raised her hands again to scratch his face; and

again to gibe at him, and to screech as if in triumph over him, that Miss Arnold already knew all, and that the cruel murder would not aid him a bit in keeping the secret about the stolen miniature.

Amid the many bitter agonies that relentless memory carried back to him of the past night, throwing a new and intense light over it all, and so bringing out into minute detail every particle of every incident that had occurred, making each appear more vividly and distinctly than it had done at the moment it happened, there was that one, beyond all the rest, which shook his coward soul with ever-increasing apprehensions ; and that was the half-smothered declaration of the strangling woman, that she had already denounced him and his theft to Agnes Arnold.

If that declaration were true, then he had, by the double murders he had committed, rendered his position more perilous, and his union with Agnes Arnold an absolute impossibility ! Then, the double murders were not only gratuitous and useless deeds of blood ; but their perpetration had brought upon himself instantaneous corporal punishment which disqualified him from carrying out, for the time, his long-matured plans both against his uncle and Miss Arnold. He did not regret the crimes, because they were crimes ; but he writhed with rage to think that if the old woman told him the truth, then the committal of those crimes was, as regarded his projects, and the assurrance of his speedy success, the very things he ought not to have done! And when such reflections overwhelmed him, he seemed to see, as his face burned, and his back smarted with pain, the widow Kinchela and her death-distorted staring eyes, and her long, fearful, blood-dripping nails, and she mouthing and mocking at him, as he tossed about in agony and despair in the dark, cold, and gloomy night.

The murderer was alone, keeping his first night watch !

Time and its progress were unheeded—the deep heavy breathing of his sleeping confederate was unnoticed—even the sounds of the returning carriage, though heard, were unattended to by the maimed and disfigured miscreant, as he lay in the midst of his own guilty reflections, and dreaded to think, not that he had committed two murders, but that those murders might, perchance, have marred, instead of having promoted his selfish and diabolical projects against his uncle's life, and Agnes Arnold's happiness.

Chapter XIV.

THE SURPRISE.

Suddenly—whilst the Lieutenant's whole being seemed to be absorbed in such bitter, torturing, and vain reflections—his faculties and his fears were restored—as through the sharp, tingling, sudden stroke of an electrical shock—by a loud, decisive knocking, outside his door.

At the same instant, the Lieutenant bounded out of bed, and the Red Spy started to his feet.

"What is that? Who is there?" asked the Lieutenant, whilst his voice trembled, in spite of himself, with fear; and his teeth chattered, as if he was suffering from intense cold.

"It is I, Master James, your own servant, Thomas."

"Go away, you scoundrel! How dare you come to me without being called? How dare

you knock at my door at this hour of the night?
You must be drunk, you rascal! I have a great
mind to open the door, and drag you into the
room, and horsewhip you, whilst able to stand
over you. Go away! go away! you filthy sot."

" Oh, you may say what you like, or do what
you wish with me, Master James; but for all
that I must obey the master's orders.'

" The master's orders! What! you blun-
dering, tippling rascal, do you mean to tell
me that it is by Mr. Kirwan's orders you are
awakening me out of my sleep at this hour of the
night?"

" Yes, sir—no, sir."

" Yes, sir! no, sir! you are very drunk,
Thomas. It is plain you do not know what you
are saying. Go away! go to bed, sirrah!"

"I am not a bit drunk, Master James; but
I am obeying the master's orders."

•• Did Mr. Kirwan order you to come here at
this hour of the night to me?"

" No, sir."

" Then, you infernally stupid scoundrel, what
brings you here?"

" The master's orders, sir."

" Why, you said this moment he did not order you to come here."

" No more he didn't, sir."

" Then, why have you knocked at the door ?"

" I couldn't help it, sir."

" Could not help it !　What do you mean ?"

" Why, sir, the master's orders were that I and all the servants in the house were to do whatever the Doctor desired us to do—and, of course, when the Doctor ordered me never to stop knocking at your door, until I got you out of bed, and into the middle of the floor, of course, I must obey his orders; because his orders, you see, Master James, are all as one as the master's orders; and that is the reason I am here, and that I must go on *tatthering* at this door here until you tell me you are standing on the floor; and, therefore, you see, Master James, I am not a bit drunk, but as sober as one of the holy wells of Listoomiavarah which never had anything in the inside of them, but cold water."

" So ! the Doctor sent you at this hour of the night to knock at my door ! "

"He did, indeed, sir. Are you out of bed, Master James?"

"I am. Why do you ask?"

"And standing upright, in the middle of the floor?"

"Yes, yes. Why so?"

"Because the Doctor told me, if knocking with my knuckles did not waken you out of your sleep, I was to go on kicking with my heels, as hard as I could pelt, ever, ever until I got you clean out of bed, and standing on the floor."

"The Doctor ordered you so to conduct yourself, Thomas?"

"As sure as I am a sinner, he did, Master James."

"Very well! very well! This matter requires explanation—not from you, Thomas; but from the Doctor. I may have to speak to him about it."

"Faith! and he may have to speak to you too, Master James; and that brings me to the message he ordered me to give you: but you are sure, Master James, you are not in bed, and you

are sure you are standing in the middle of the
floor."

"Yes, yes, stupid! Now, what is the important message you have to deliver to me from
the Doctor, at this unseasonable hour of the
night ? "

"Why, then, Master James, it is just like
what all doctors' messages ought to be. It is
very short, very simple, very intelligible, and very
easy to be remembered. It is, Master James,
that he—that is the Doctor—knows very well
what is the matter with you—that is yourself,
Master James, and, therefore he, that is the
Doctor—knows that it will be very dangerous for
you—that is yourself, Master James—and very
probably for others (but who they are I don't know)
if you—that is yourself, Master James—were to
remain in this house, until morning ; and, therefore, that he—the Doctor—has ordered that a
gig, or chaise, or horse should be got ready for
you to start in a quarter of an hour from this
time. And the Doctor desired me to add,
Master James, that he will be coming up to your
room, in five minutes after I go down stairs—and

that he has some important medical advice to give you, but insists upon speaking to you alone—and he desired me to repeat the word three times to you—'alone, alone, alone!' That is all I have to say to you, Master James, except to ask, what do you wish me to get ready for you?—a horse, a gig, or a chaise?"

"Wait a minute, Thomas," replied the Lieutenant, as he looked with fear and trembling at the Red Spy.

"Of course, I'll wait a minute, Master James, because I was not ordered, not to wait a minute," was the polite reply given by Thomas, outside the door.

"What say you, Reddy, to this strange—this ominous message? that 'he knows what is the matter with me,' and that 'it is dangerous' for me to remain in the house a quarter of an hour longer?"

"Whatever it means, act on it?" replied Reddy. "Whether the Doctor knows all, or a little, or nothing at all, still with your face in its present condition you cannot remain here. You were yourself thinking of leaving the house. Your enemies are doing for you what you intended

to do for yourself.   Say that you will go ; and
that you will see the Doctor."

"See the Doctor !   With this face !   Why,
if he knows or suspects the truth, it will convict
me," observed the broken-spirited Lieutenant.

"No matter ! he *will* see you, whether you
like it or not ; and you ought to be aware of what
is against you, especially as the time and opportunity for running away are given you."

"Be it so," answered the Lieutenant, with a
heavy sigh.   "Thomas," he added addressing
the servant outside.   "Let my uncle's gig be at
the door in a quarter of an hour, and do not you,
or any of the servants come near me ; for I am
afraid I have got the small-pock."

"I am   heartily   sorry   to   hear   it   Master
James,—and if you have it, the Lord send
you safe through with it.   It is the wicked alone,
Master James, ought to be afflicted in that way ;
for as to the good, they are sure of having crosses
and contradictions enough in life without the
affliction of any such horrid disease.   The Lord
preserve you ! Master James ; for it is you, that
are the good man's nephew ; and for his sake, as

well as your own, I wish you safe and sound, soul and body, Master James."

" Thank you, Thomas, for your good wishes; but mind you do not attempt to come near me when I am going away."

" Oh ! certainly not, Master James, as you order me not. I am always for obeying orders. But what am I to say to the Doctor about seeing him alone?—he said 'he must see you alone, alone, alone.' These are his very words over again."

"That he shall see me alone, in five minutes. And remember, Thomas, that you say to him—I expect to see him in his professional capacity as a Doctor."

" ' Professional capacity as a Doctor !' ' professional capacity as a Doctor !' They are very hard words, Master James; but I will try and remember them ! and I'll be off at once, for fear I should forget them, you will find the gig with the grey mare, your favorite roadster, at the door in a quarter of an hour," said Thomas hurrying off, and repeating to himself, as he descended the stairs—' professional capacity as a Doctor !'

" By using these words," observed the Lieutenant to the Red Spy, " I impose secrecy upon the doctor—because he cannot disclose against me what he has observed in treating with me as my physican.　And now. Reddy—be off!—meet me at the first milestone outside the park, on the road to Dublin.　I can there tell you what has passed between me and this meddling quack ; and we can then concert our future measures together—and you either travel with me, or remain behind ; whichever you deem to be most advisable."

" I'm off, like a shot," replied the Red Spy ; " but I hope you will allow me, Master James, to put the whiskey bottle and the little that remains of it, in one pocket, and the bottle of brandy in the other.　It would almost break my heart to quit this place, and leave such liquor behind me."

" Do as you like," answered the Lieutenant. "Take care, however, you are not observed leaving the house."

" I never go out by a door, if it is more convenient, and less liable to interruption to skulk away through a window," said the Spy, as he quitted the room.

The Lieutenant arranged the lights, which had been burning on the table, in a distant corner of the room, so that his face should be completely shaded in the place where he took his seat—at the side of the bed—and where the overhanging curtains might, as far as possible, conceal his head and shoulders.

In this position he awaited, with a beating heart, and trembling limbs, the entrance of the physican. At length that gentleman's knock was heard, and the Lieutenant desired him to open the door and come in.

The door opened, and as it did so a bright light shone into the apartment. In the centre of this light stood for a moment Doctor Devitt— gleams resting and flashing on the two polished barrels of a pistol he held in his right hand.

The Doctor closed the door, and said : " I have placed lights outside to deter any spy from approaching the door, and overhearing our conversation. I also wished, at once, to make you aware, Lieutenant Williams, that I come prepared to repel force by force ; and that to your instan-

tancous and inevitable destruction, in case you
should be mad enough or wicked enough to
resort to any act of violence."

" You wish to see me, sir," replied the Lieutenant, " as I understand in your professional
capacity. Wherefore ? "

" Because," said the physician, "I believe
you require the aid of my medical skill at this
moment. I do not desire, Lieutenant Williams,
to intrude upon you with my advice ; and I am
rather pleased to find that you have purposely
placed yourself in a position, in which, it is impossible for me to see your face. I do not desire
to look at it. On the contrary I want not to see
it ; nor to ascertain whether any accident has
befallen you during the past night."

" Then, wherefore have you come to me at
this unseasonable hour ?" said the Lieutenant in
an impertinent and blustering tone of voice, the
effect of which was somewhat marred by a slight
tremor and hesitation in his speech.

" Not for your sake sir, be assured of that ;
but for the sake of that best of human beings,
your uncle, John Kirwan. I have come to you,

Sir, because I have this night been at the cottage of the widow Kinchela, and from an examination of the body, can depose on oath that she was strangled in her bed. My experience, too, as a medical man, enables me to say that her death was preceded by a very desperate struggle ; and that whoever was her assassin, she tore his face in many places ; for although there was no effusion of blood from her person, the sheets, the bolster, and the pillow are spotted with blood—and that blood plainly dripped from the countenance of the vile murderer, whilst he was choking her. I believe, too, that every juror of the County Wexford must come to the same conclusion as to who was her murderer. They must—from the evidence supplied by himself—fix the guilt of this most cruel murder upon one man—one man alone in the entire county."

" What—what—what do you mean Doctor Devitt? I do not understand you. What evidence of his own guilt could the murderer have left behind him ?" stammered out the Lieutenant.

" His own hair, Sir," replied the Doctor—" Short, curly, wooly hair—found in the closed hand of the deceased. There is but one person in the whole county has such hair; and a very few hours before her death, the deceased expressed to two credible witnesses, her apprehension that she would be murdered in her bed, by that very person who has the remarkable hair. A short time after her death, that same person with the peculiar hair was seen coming from the widow's cottage, was pursued, was fired at, was wounded, and was distinctly recognised by the person who wounded him."

" Who told you that, Doctor?"

" The man himself!" replied Doctor Devitt.

" The man himself! Why he is dead," involuntarily remarked the Lieutenant.

" He was left for dead—but he is not dead," said Doctor Devitt. " The mercy of Providence preserved his life ; and he is living, and will, in a few days, be so far recovered, as to give evidence in a court of justice. There, he will name, amid the horror and execration of every human being, the murderer of the widow Kinchela. And now, sir, to tell you the purport of my visit. A messenger has been despatched for the Coroner

of the County. He will be here in the course
of a few hours. The facts I have mentioned will
be sworn to. Upon the statement of these facts,
a warrant will inevitably be issued for your
apprehension ; and I wish to spare your good
uncle the pain and horror of seeing you arrested
as a murderer. If your face be uninjured by a
scratch, you will remain : if your body be un-
touched by a gun-shot wound you will not stir ;
because then the circumstances that will serve to
bring home the crime to the murderer will not
apply to you. And now, sir, I have done with
you. I have come to give you medical advice.
Considering the circumstances I have mentioned,
and that have come to my knowledge, I am the
very last person whose professional assistance you
should seek. I advise you then, as a physican,
to go to Wexford or Dublin—see a medical man
in either place as soon as you can—and when you
have recovered your health, fly—on the instant—
out of Europe—bury yourself, your name, your
shame, and your guilt in the wilds of Asia, or
the deserts of Africa ; and let all who are dis-
honoured by connection or acquaintanceship with

you, forget that there ever existed a monster so cruel, so base, and so infamous as yourself. Go, sir! Quit your uncle's house instantly. It is contaminated by your presence. Go, sir! and if there remain one tiny spark of the gentleman in your callous heart, think over these lines of the old English poet, and—act upon them :—

" Now must I hang myself : my friends will look
    for 't :
Eating and sleeping I do despise you both now.
I will run mad first, and if that get not pity,
I'll drown myself to a most doleful ditty."

CHAPTER XV.

LOVE AND POETRY.

FOUR weeks had passed away since Lieutenant Williams had fled, a self-banished man, from the house of his uncle.

During that period of time his half-brother, John, had been slowly recovering from the wounds he had received, when defending Miss Arnold from the attempt at abduction made by Captain Hepenstall, at the instigation of the Lieutenant.

John's progress to convalescence, though slow, was still considerably promoted by the happiness he enjoyed in the society of Agnes ; and it was now so far advanced that he was, with the permission of the Doctor, carried down to the drawing-room, where he usually remained from mid-day until evening.

The arrangements of the family, when John

was thus conveyed to the drawing-room, were invariably the same. A table, covered with books and drawing materials, was placed close to a window commanding an extensive view of the park and avenue leading up to the front of the house. At this table was seated John ; and opposite to him was a chair, almost constantly occupied by Agnes, whilst near to her, but seated at another table, and fronting another window, was Lucy, with work-boxes, needle-cases, and other implements of feminine industry. On the left-hand side of John was an arm-chair for the doctor, when he visited his patient. And there, if the doctor was not present, sat Mr. Kirwan, whenever he was not engaged in his usual in-door exercise—walking slowly, with his hands behind his back, from one end of the drawing-room to the other.

Upon the particular day, on which occurred the events we are about to describe, John was at the table, with an open book in his hand, and Agnes was engaged in conversation with him. Lucy sat silent, busily engaged over a piece of work she had in hand, and it was manifest from the rapidity with which she plied her needle, that she was desirous to have it finished as soon as possible. This piece of work was a dark frock for a child. Lucy herself was clothed in black, and so were Agnes and John.

The low, murmuring conversation of John and Agnes could scarcely be heard. It was so soft and so gentle, it certainly did not in the slightest degree interfere with the meditation in which old John Kirwan was indulging as he paced, with a heavy heart and a slow step, from end to end of the drawing-room.

Four weeks had produced a great change in the appearance of John Kirwan. The liveliness and vivacity of his manner had altogether disappeared. His hair had assumed a white hue, and was considerably thinned, whilst his shoulders had become more stooped, and his head sank lower and heavier over his breast; and the eyes, which before used to sparkle with benevolence, seemed now to gaze vacantly around him, as if he saw not what he appeared to look at, or, as if his mind was altogether engaged in the contemplation of painful and embittering thoughts.

John Kirwan was unwittingly falling into a

great error. He was yielding himself a prey to grief at the very time he had fancied he was struggling manfully against it; and when he supposed he was acting as a martyr, he was, in fact, allowing himself to become a victim. The mistake is a very common one; for with the great majority of mankind, their feelings and passions are stronger than their powers of reasoning. Let us listen to the sensitive self-tormentor as he communes with himself—alone with his own heart—and unconscious of the love that glances from every eye in that drawing-room upon him.

"What a fool! What a fool! What a fool!—I have been? I thought that by doing my duty—more than my duty to others, I thereby secured their love—their respect—their gratitude! Fool! I supposed that by never intentionally speaking an untruth of others I thereby rendered myself impregnable against the assault of calumny, and the attacks of malevolence. Idiot! I imagined that by being open-hearted with others I thereby made for myself a shield against treachery. How have I mistaken my position? How little did I know of the world in which I

have been so long living, when he—the man
beyond all others—who should have stood by my
side when dangers beset or perils surrounded
me—should have acted as the ally of my enemies ;
and should have shown them how—if it were
possible — to reduce me from competency to
beggary.

" What ! my nephew ! my own nephew ! he,
in whose veins flow my own blood ! my brother's
son !—to turn against me !—to plot against my
life !—and in sustainment of that plot to murder
my old nurse—my play-fellow in childhood !
Oh ! Heavens ! was there ever such a combina-
tion of blood-thirsty treachery as has been
directed against me ! Was there ever such baseness and ingratitude ! But—no matter ! no
matter !—I *will* bear it as a man, and—as a
Christian ! I will not repine ; I will remember
that mine is the lot of humanity ; and that all
such afflictions are sent for our good ; and that
we ought to submit to them with meekness ; and
that we ought not to desire anything else but
such crosses and contradictions ; for these are the
very words of dear old Thomas-à-Kempis :—

" ' Erras, erras, si aliud quaeris quam pati tribulationes ; quia tota ista vita mortalis plena est miseriis, et circumsignata crucibus.'

" Yes ! yes ! that is the saying of a wise man. Every one—and why not I too !—we are all in error, in a sad error, whenever we look for, or expect anything here, but sorrow and trouble ; for human life is crowded with calamities and staked round with afflictions.

"And yet, what a booby I am ! The truth of that saying (and I knew it years ago as well as I now know it) never occurred to me until my nephew James became a traitor, a thief, and a murderer. The infernal miscreant ! How could he have the heart so to behave towards me ? What act was there of mine to him, but one marked with generosity ? What word of mine to him, but what was impressed with affection ? If I had conducted myself as a selfish man—if I had shut my door in his face, when he first arrived in Ireland from Jamaica—then he never could have had the opportunity of injuring me ; or, if he had made the attempt, my heart would not be filled with gall and bitterness against myself, as a dupe; nor against him for assailing me.

"But, no! no. This has not been the treatment I expected: this is not the return I calculated upon. Oh! this world! this world! See how it goes on, smiling, and jocund, and the sun shining as brightly, and the birds singing as sweetly, as if ingratitude was not converting it into a hell; and the persecution of the innocent by the wicked making it more rotten, foul, and loathsome than a charnel-house! What business has a man with pure motives and honest intentions, to live any longer amid such a gang of miscreants! Oh! for the grave! the peaceful grave! the quiet, undisturbed grave where the eye would be shut and the ear closed for ever to the deeds and wōrds of a traitor—like James, and a craven—like Hepenstall.

"I am wrong—I am wrong. The pack of rascals! Although they have rendered life not only distasteful, but odious to me, still I would not like to die just yet—I would not like to give the scoundrels the comfort of thinking that their machinations had power to kill me—to

break my heart.   If I could, I would not let them
even guess, that their villany had deprived me
of an hours sleep.

"The unfeeling, base miscreants have made
me miserable—very miserable; but still—I will
bear up against it all.   I will endeavour to think
that these tribulations are sent to me for my
good; and—when a mightier bitterness of spirit
than ordinary falls upon me, I shall again have
recourse to Thomas-à-Kempis, and console
myself; and strengthen myself with this blessed
sentence :—

"'Etiam si poenas et verbera dederit, gratum
esse debet, quia semper pro salute nostra facit,
quicquid nobis advenire permittit.'"

And so went on, hour after hour, poor John
Kirwan, eating out his own heart with his sad
reflections.   He foolishly supposed he was over-
coming his tender nature and lacerated feelings,
by repetition of most wise maxims : maxims that
only left a temporary impression upon his mind ;
because they were not embraced with sufficient
ardour ; nor adopted with such a firm resolution
as to form a permanent rule for his conduct.

His strength lay in his memory and his words, and not in his will, nor his actions. He was his own moral director; and he was therefore, for ever oscillating between sensitiveness, of which he had too much, and fortitude, of which he had not sufficient.

Whilst John Kirwan was thus communing in bitter sadness with himself, a short, interesting, but eventful conversation, took place between Agnes and his nephew, which originated in an accidental reference to two old English dramatic poets.

" I observe," said Agnes, " you have a book open before you, Mr. Kirwan Williams. Is it the same work you were reading yesterday ? "

" It is, Miss Arnold. I am delighted with it. The more I read the plays of Beaumont and Fletcher, the more I am charmed—almost fascinated with them. There are some exquisitely tender and beautiful passages in their compositions. A few, so very beautiful, they appear to have been written by Shakspeare. Here, for instance, are three lines, descriptive of a young

N 3

maiden—worthy, I think, of being printed in letters of gold."

"They must be very fine, I am sure," said Agnes, "when you so praise them."

"Listen to them," said John. "I fancy, Miss Arnold, as I read them, that I see the original before me—

        "'Her sweet humour
That is as easy as a calm, and peaceful;
All her affections like the dews on roses,
Fair as the flowers themselves, as sweet and
       gentle.'"

"Very pretty lines, indeed, Mr. Kirwan Williams," said Agnes. "Are there any more passages of the same description?"

"Oh! several, Miss Arnold. What, for instance can be more pastoral and tender than this declaration of love, made by a poor shepherd to his mistress?

        "'Oh! you are fairer far
Than the chaste blushing morning, or that fair
       star

That guides the wand'ring seaman thro' the deep.
Straighter than straightest pine upon the steep
Head of an aged mountain ; and more white
Than the new milk we strip before day-light
From the full-freighted bags of our fair flocks ;
Your hair more beauteous than those hanging locks
Of young Apollo.' "

Lucy's needle ceased, and an arch smile wreathed around her rosy lips, as she looked at the reader of poetry and his attentive auditor.

"One quotation more, Miss Arnold, if you please," said John. "It is the description of a lover to his lady, who is doubtful whether or not her charms have captivated him. Would you have any objection to my reading this very sweet passage for you ? "

"I! an objection ! Certainly not, I admire your reading very much. You seem to feel what you read."

John bowed to the compliment, and then read the following lines :—

" If it be love
To forget all respect for his friends

By thinking of your face; if it be love,
'To sit cross-arm'd and sigh away the day,
Mingl'd with starts, crying your name as loud
And hastily as men i' th' streets do fire;
If it be love to weep himself away,
When he but hears of any lady dead,
Or kill'd, because it might have been your
    chance ;
Or when he goes to rest, (which will not be)
T'wixt ev'ry prayer he says, to name you once,
As others drop a bead, be to be in love,
Then, madam, I dare swear he loves you."

Agnes marked the deep emotion of the reader
as he recited aloud the preceding passages, and,
as he concluded the last lines, she fixed her full
dark eyes upon him. He looked up from the
book as he had concluded. Their glances met,
and at the same instant the checks of both were
suffused with a deep blush.

Lucy had ceased sewing, and looked alternately
from Agnes to John, as if expecting that all this
poetry would be followed by some decisive demon-
stration.

"Have you ever read, Miss Arnold," said

John, endeavouring to cover his emotion by an indifferent question " any of the plays of Beaumont and Fletcher ? "

" I only know one of them by name ; and from that I have read some extracts which pleased me greatly," replied Agnes.

" What is the name of the play ? " asked John.

" The *Elder* Brother," answered Agnes, " I admire the plot of it also. I know of no nobler passage in any poet, than that in which *Charles*— the scholar—the brave youth—the accomplished gentleman—upon discovering the beauty and worth of *Angelina*, repudiates the pretensions of his younger brother, and asserts to herself by the strength of his affections his right to her hand."

" Oh ! it is splendid !" said John, his eyes sparkling with delight, " I have the passage off by heart. I wish you knew the response of the lady."

" Recite your part," said Agnes, smiling, " Perhaps what you say may recall to my memory the line *Angelina* has to speak."

" 'Thus it is," said John, " *Charles* addresses
Angelina—

" Can you love for love and make that the reward ?
The old man shall not love his heaps of gold
With a more doating superstition,
Than I'll love you; the young man his delights ;
The merchant when he ploughs the angry sea up,
And sees the mountain-billows falling on him,
As if all the elements and all their angers,
Were turn'd into one vow'd destruction,
Shall not with greater joy embrace his safety.
We'll live together like two wanton vines,
Curling our souls and loves in one another ;
We'll spring together, and we'll bear one fruit,
One joy shall make us smile, and one grief
    mourn,
One age go with us, and one hour of death,
Shall close our eyes, and one grave make us
    happy."

Agnes leaned across the table, and placing
her fair right hand in that of Kirwan William's,
said :—

" And one hand seal the match. I'm your's for ever."

The young barrister clasped the hand of the lady; and in that pressure was the first ratification to the first declaration of love between the nephew and the ward of John Kirwan.

And John Kirwan was in the room all the the time; and in his ears was murmured all this poetry, and before his eyes was this clasping of hands; and yet he heard nothing, saw nothing, and knew nothing of it all; for he was thinking of present griefs and past transactions—his time was uselessly passing away, wasted between a fretful memory, and objectless reflections!

The smiling, silent Lucy had heard and seen what has been described; and she appeared to think she now knew all that it was necessary to be sure of; and she therefore returned to her work, and plied her needle with fresh and vigorous activity.

END OF VOL II.

30, Welbeck Street,
Cavendish Square,
1860.

MR. NEWBY'S
NEW PUBLICATIONS.

I.

In 2 vols., post 8vo., price 21s.,

FRIENDS FOR THE FIRESIDE.

By MRS. MATHEWS,

Author of "Memoirs of Charles Mathews," "Tea Table Talk," &c.

Recollections—Anecdote and Joke—Notings—Selections—
With Gravities for Grave Folk.

II.

In 2 vols., post 8vo., price 21s.,

AN OLD ROAD AND AN OLD RIVER.

By W. ROSS,

Author of a "Yacht Voyage to Norway, Sweden, Denmark," &c.

III.

In 1 vol., post 8vo., price 10s. 6d.,

FROM EVE TILL MORN IN EUROPE.

By MRS. AGAR,

Author of "Knights of the Cross," &c.

IV.

In 1 vol., post 8vo., price 10s. 6d.,

DEAFNESS AND DISEASES OF THE EAR.

The Fallacies and Present Treatment Exposed, and Remedies
suggested from the experience of half a century.

By W. WRIGHT, ESQ.,

Surgeon Aurist (by Royal Sign Manual) to her late Majesty
Queen Charlotte.

V.

In 1 vol., fcap. 8vo., price 2s.,

THOMAS MOORE, HIS LIFE AND WRITINGS.

By H. MONTGOMERY, ESQ.

VI.

In 1 vol., post 8vo., price 7s. 6d. (*with Map*),

FIVE YEARS IN THE FREE STATES OF AMERICA.

By W. HANCOCK, Esq.

VII.

DEDICATED TO THE OFFICERS AND PRIVATES OF THE
VOLUNTEER SERVICE.

In 1 vol., post 8vo., price 10s. 6d.,

PERILS AND PANICS OF INVASION,

In 1796–7–8, and 1804–5, and at the Present Time.

By HUMPHREY BLUNT.

VIII.

In 2 vols., post 8vo., price 21s.,

CURIOUS THINGS OF THE OUTSIDE WORLD.

By HARGRAVE JENNINGS.

IX.

In 2 vols., price 21s. (*Second Edition*),

AMERICAN PHOTOGRAPHS.

By the MISSES TURNBULL.

" It is exceedingly amusing, and marked by energy and power."
—*Globe.*

"Twenty-six thousand miles of travel, by two young ladies, in
search of the new, the beautiful, and the instructive! We do not
know that a reader could desire more amusing *compagnons de voyage*
than these two sprightly, intelligent, well-educated, and observant
young Englishwomen."—*Morning Advertiser.*

"A number of amusing anecdotes give life and interest to the
narrative."—*Brighton Examiner.*

"Very pleasant gossipping volumes."—*Critic.*

"These volumes are replete with lively, entertaining sketches of
American manners and customs, sayings and doings."—*Naval and
Military.*

"Contains much information respecting the manners and habits
of our transatlantic cousins."—*Sun.*

"The narrative is evidently truthful, as it is clear and intelligible."—*Herald.*

X.

In 1 vol., price 5s.,

SPIRITUALISM, AND THE AGE WE LIVE IN.

By CATHARINE CROWE,
Author of "The Night Side of Nature," "Ghost Stories," &c.

XI.

In 2 vols., post 8vo., price 21s.,

MY FIRST TRAVELS;

Including Rides in the Pyrenees; Scenes during an Inundation at Avignon; Sketches in France and Savoy; Visits to Convents and Houses of Charity, &c. &c.

By SELINA BUNBURY.

" A remarkably readable book, full of life and colour, and invested with a dramatic interest rarely to be met with in works of its class. The book is impressed with the freshness of youth and the artistic skill of maturity."—*Globe.*

" These Travels must meet with a favourable reception."—*Ladies' Review.*

" Miss Bunbury is both instructive and entertaining. There is a freshness combined with sterling good sense."—*Express.*

XII.

In 1 vol., post 8vo., price 10s. 6d.,

OUR PLAGUE SPOT:

In connection with our Polity and Usages as regards our Women, our Soldiery, and the Indian Empire.

XIII.

In 1 vol., price 10s. 6d.,

SUNDAY, THE REST OF LABOUR.

DEDICATED TO THE ARCHBISHOP OF CANTERBURY.

"This important subject is discussed ably and temperately; and though many differences will arise in the minds of some of our clergy, as well as some pious laymen, it should be added to every library."—*Herald.*

" Written by a churchman, who is evidently a man with deep and sincere religious feelings. His book is temperately written, and will have a wholesome tendency, if wisely received."—*Examiner.*

XIV.

In 1 vol., price 2s. 6d.,

DRAWING-ROOM CHARADES FOR ACTING.

By C. WARREN ADAMS, Esq.

"A valuable addition to Christmas diversions. It consists of a number of well-constructed scenes for charades."—*Guardian.*

XV.

In 1 vol., price 12s.,

MERRIE ENGLAND.

By LORD WILLIAM LENNOX.

"It overflows with racy, poignant anecdotes of a generation just passed away. The book is destined to lie upon the tables of many a country mansion."—*Leader.*

XVI.

In 1 vol., price 5s.,

KNIGHTS OF THE CROSS.

By MRS. AGAR.

"Nothing can be more appropriate than this little volume, from which the young will learn how their forefathers venerated and fought to preserve those places hallowed by the presence of the Saviour."—*Guardian.*

"Mrs. Agar has written a book which young and old may read with profit and pleasure."—*Sunday Times.*

"It is a work of care and research, which parents may well wish to see in the hands of their children."—*Leader.*

"A well-written history of the Crusades, pleasant to read, and good to look upon."—*Critic.*

XVII.

In 1 vol., post 8vo., price 10s. 6d.,

AN AUTUMN IN SILESIA, AUSTRIA PROPER, AND THE OBER ENNS.

By the Author of "Travels in Bohemia."

XVIII.

STEPS ON THE MOUNTAINS.

"This is a step in the right way, and ought to be in the hands of the youth of both sexes."—*Review*.

"The moral of this graceful and well-constructed little tale is, that Christian influence and good example have a better effect in doing the good work of reformation than the prison, the treadmill, or even the reformatory."—*Critic*.

"The Steps on the Mountains are traced in a loving spirit. They are earnest exhortations to the sober and religious-minded to undertake the spiritual and temporal improvement of the condition of the destitute of our lanes and alleys. The moral of the tale is well carried out; and the bread which was cast upon the waters is found after many days, to the saving and happiness of all therein concerned."—*Athenæum*.

XIX.

In 1 vol., post 8vo., price 10s. 6d.,

ZEAL IN THE WORK OF THE MINISTRY.

By L'ABBE DUBOIS.

"There is a tone of piety and reality in the work of l'Abbe Dubois, and a unity of aim, which is to fix the priest's mind on the duties and responsibilities of his whole position, and which we admire. The writer is occupied supremely with one thought of contributing to the salvation of souls and to the glory of God."—*Literary Churchman*.

XX.

In 1 vol., price 5s.,

FISHES AND FISHING.

By W. WRIGHT, Esq.

"Anglers will find it worth their while to profit by the author's experience."—*Athenæum.*

"The pages abound in a variety of interesting anecdotes connected with the rod and the line. The work will be found both useful and entertaining to the lovers of the piscatory art."—*Morning Post.*

"It is both amusing and instructive."—*Daily Telegraph.*

"A pleasant and gossipping book on the subject, with authentic facts gleaned from sources which could be depended upon, and worthy to be remembered, relative to angling in all its branches."—*Lancet.*

XXI.

In 1 vol., price 10s. 6d.,

THE NEW EL DORADO;

OR, BRITISH COLUMBIA.

By KINAHAN CORNWALLIS.

"The book is full of information as to the best modes existing or expected of reaching these enviable countries."—*Morning Chronicle.*

"The book gives all the information which it is possible to obtain respecting the new colony called British Columbia. The book is altogether one of a most interesting and instructive character."—*The Star.*

"The work is very spiritedly written, and will amuse and instruct."—*Observer.*

XXII.

In 1 vol., price 10s. 6d.,

NIL DESPERANDUM,

BEING AN ESCAPE FROM ITALIAN DUNGEONS.

"We find the volume entertaining, and really Italian in spirit."
—*Athenæum*.

"There is much fervour in this romantic narrative of suffering."
—*Examiner*.

XXIII.

In 2 vols., post 8vo., price 21s.,

A PANORAMA OF THE NEW WORLD.

By KINAHAN CORNWALLIS,

Author of "Two Journeys to Japan," &c.

"Nothing can be more spirited, graphic, and full of interest, nothing more pictorial or brilliant in its execution and animation."
—*Globe*.

"One of the most amusing tales ever written."—*Review*.

"He is a lively, rattling writer. The sketches of Peruvian Life and Manners are fresh, racy, and vigorous. The volumes abound with amusing anecdotes and conversations."—*Weekly Mail*.

XXIV.

In 1 vol., 8vo., price 10s. 6d.,

LIFE OF ALEXANDER THE FIRST.

By IVAN GOLOVIN.

"It is a welcome contribution to Russian imperial biography."—*Leader*.

"Mr. Golovin possesses fresher information, a fresher mind and manner applied to Russian affairs, than foreigners are likely to possess."—*Spectator*.

30, WELBECK STREET, CAVENDISH
SQUARE, LONDON.

MR. NEWBY'S
NEW PUBLICATIONS.

I.

In 2 vols. post 8vo., price 21s.

FRIENDS FOR THE FIRESIDE,

BY MRS. MATHEWS,

Author of "Memoirs of Charles Mathews," "Tea
Table Talk,"

Recollections, Anecdote, and Joke,
Notings, Selections, with Gravities for Grave Folk.

II.

In 2 vols., post 8vo., price 21s.

AN OLD ROAD AND AN OLD RIVER,

BY WILLIAM A. ROSS,

Author of "A Yatch·Voyage to Norway, Sweeden,
and Denmark."

III.

In 1 vol. post 8vo., price 10s. 6d.

PERILS AND PANICS

Of Volunteers and Invasions in 1796-7-8, 1805, and at
the Present Time,

BY HUMPHREY BLUNT.

IV.

In 1 vol., post 8vo., plates, price 10s. 6d.

DEAFNESS & DISEASES OF THE EAR,

The Fallacies of present treatment exposed and Remedies
suggested from the experience of half-a-century,

BY W. WRIGHT, Esq.

Surgeon Aurist (by Royal Sign Manual,) to Her
Majesty, the late Queen Charlotte, &c.

V.

In 1 vol., post 8vo. with map, price 7s. 6d.

AN EMIGRANT'S FIVE YEARS IN THE FREE STATES OF AMERICA,

BY WILLIAM HANCOCK.

VI.

In 1 vol. crown 8vo., price 2s.

THOMAS MOORE—HIS LIFE AND WRITINGS,

BY HENRY MONTGOMERY, ESQ.

VII.

In 1 vol. post 8vo., price 10s. 6d.

FROM MORN TILL EVE IN EUROPE,

BY MRS. AGAR,

Author of "The Knights of the Cross," &c.

VIII.

In 1 vol. post 8vo., price 5s.

SPIRITUALISM AND THE AGE WE LIVE IN,

BY MRS. CROWE,

Author of "The Night Side of Nature," "Ghost
Stories, &c.

IX.

In 2 vols., price 21s.

AMERICAN PHOTOGRAPHS,

BY THE MISSES TURNBULL.

"It is exceedingly amusing, and marked by energy and power.'
—*Globe*.

"Twenty-six thousand miles of travel by two young ladies, in search of the new, the beautiful, and the instructive! We do not know that a reader could desire more amusing *compagnons de voyage* than these two sprightly, intelligent, well-educated, and observant young Englishwomen."—*Morning Advertiser*.

"A number of amusing anecdotes give life and interest to the narrative."—*Brighton Examiner*.

"Very pleasant gosipping volumes."—*Critic*. .

"These volumes are replete with lively, entertaining sketches of American manners and customs, sayings and doings."—*Naval and Military*.

"Contains much information respecting the manners and habits of our transatlantic cousins."—*Sun*.

"The narrative is evidently truthful, as it is clear and intelligible."—*Herald*.

X.

In 1 vol. post 8vo., price 10s. 6d.

OUR PLAGUE SPOT,

In connection with our Polity and Usages as regards Women, our Soldiery, and the Indian Empire.

XI.

In 1 vol., price 10s. 6d.

SUNDAY, THE REST OF LABOUR,

Dedicated to the Archbishop of Canterbury.

"This important subject is discussed ably and temperately; and though many differences will arise in the minds of some of our clergy, as well as some pious laymen, it should be added to every library."—*Herald*.

"Written by a churchman, who is evidently a man with deep and sincere religious feelings. His book is temperately written, and will have a wholesome tendency, if wisely received."—*Exam*.

XII.

In 1 vol., price 2s. 6d.

DRAWING-ROOM CHARADES FOR ACTING,

BY C. WARREN ADAMS, Esq.

"A valuable addition to Christmas diversions It consists of a number of well-constructed scenes for charades."—*Guardian.*

XIII.

In 1 vol., price 12s.

MERRIE ENGLAND,

BY LORD WILLIAM LENNOX.

"It overflows with racy, picqant anecdotes of a generation just passed away. The book is destined to lie upon the tables of many a country mansion."—*Leader.*

XIV.

In 1 vol., price 5s.

KNIGHTS OF THE CROSS,

BY MRS. AGAR.

" Nothing can be more appropriate than this little volume, from which the young will learn how their forefathers venerated and fought to preserve those places hallowed by the presence of the Saviour "—*Guardian.*

"Mrs. Agar has written a book which young and old may read with profit and pleasure."—*Sunday Times.*

"It is a work of care and research, which parents may well wish to see in the hands of their children."—*Leader.*

"A well-written history of the Crusades, pleasant to read, and good to look upon."—*Critic.*

XV.

In 1 vol. post 8vo., price 10s. 6d.

AN AUTUMN IN SILESIA, AUSTRIA PROPER, AND THE OBER ENNS,

By the Author of " Travels in Bohemia."

XVI.

STEPS ON THE MOUNTAINS.

"This is a step in the right way, and ought to be in the hands of the youth of both sexes."—*Review.*

"The moral of this graceful and well-constructed little tale is, that Christian influence and good example have a better effect in doing the good work of reformation than the prison, the treadmill, or either the reformatory."—*Critic.*

"The Steps on the Mountains are traced in a loving spirit. They are earnest exhortations to the sober and religious-minded to undertake the spiritual and temporal improvement of the condition of the destitute of our lanes and alleys. The moral of the tale is well carried out; and the bread which was cast upon the waters is found after many days, to the saving and happiness of all therein concerned."—*Athenæum.*

XVII.

In 1 vol., price 5s.

FISHES AND FISHING,

BY W. WRIGHT, Esq.

"Anglers will find it worth their while to profit by the author's experience."—*Athenæum.*

"The pages abound in a variety of interesting anecdotes connected with the rod and the line. The work will be found both useful and entertaining to the lovers of the piscatory art."—*Morning Post.*

XVIII.

In 1 vol. 8vo., price 10s. 6d.

LIFE OF ALEXANDER THE FIRST,

BY IVAN GOLOVIN.

"It is a welcome contribution to Russian imperial biography."—*Leader.*

"Mr. Golovin possesses fresher information, a fresher mind and manner applied to Russian affairs, than foreigners are likely to possess."—*Spectator.*

XIX.

In 1 vol. post 8vo., price 10s. 6d.

ZEAL IN THE WORK OF THE MINISTRY,

BT L'ABBE DUBOIS.

"There is a tone of piety and reality in the work of l'Abbe Dubois, and a unity of aim, which is to fix the priest's mind on the duties and responsibilities of his whole position, and which we admire. The writer is occupied supremely with one thought of contributing to the salvation of souls and to the glory of God.— *Literary Churchman.*

"It abounds in sound and discriminating reflections and valuable hints. No portion of a Clergyman's duties is overlooked."— *The Ecclesiastic.*

"This volume enters so charmingly into the minutiæ of clerical life, that we know none so calculated to assist the young priest and direct him in his duties. It is a precious legacy of wisdom to all the priesthood."— *Union.*

XX.

In 1 vol., price 10s. 6d.

THE NEW EL DORADO; OR BRITISH COLUMBIA.

BY KINAHAN CORNWALLIS.

"The book is full of information as to the best modes existing or expected of reaching these enviable countries."— *Morning Chronicle.*

"The book gives all the information which it is possible to obtain respecting the new colony called British Columbia. The book is altogether one of a most interesting and instructive character."— *The Star.*

"The work is very spiritedly written, and will amuse and instruct."— *Observer.*

XXI.

In 2 vols. post 8vo., price 21s.

A PANORAMA OF THE NEW WORLD,

BY KINAHAN CORNWALLIS,

Author of "Two Journeys to Japan."

" Nothing can be more spirited, graphic, and full of interest, nothing more pictorial or brilliant in its execution and animation." —*Globe*.

"One of the most amusing tales ever written."—*Review*.

"He is a lively, rattling writer. The sketches of Peruvian Life and manners are fresh, racy and vigorous. The volumes abound with amusing anecdotes and conversations."—*Weekly Mail*.

XXII.

In 1 vol., price 10s. 6d.

NIL DESPERANDUM,

BEING AN ESCAPE FROM ITALIAN DUNGEONS.

"We find the volume entertaining and really Italian in spirit." —*Athenæum*.

"There is much fervour in this romantic narrative of suffering." —*Examiner*.

XXIII.

In 2 vols., price 21s.

THIRTY-FIVE YEARS OF A DRAMATIC AUTHOR'S LIFE,

BY EDWARD FITZBALL, Esq.

"We scarcely remember any biography so replete with anecdotes of the most agreeable description. Everybody in the theatrical world, and a great many out of it, figure in this admirable biography."—*Globe*.

"One of the most curious collections of histrionic incidents ever put together. Fitzball numbers his admirers not by hundreds and thousands, but by millions."—*Liverpool Albion*.

"A most wonderful book about all sorts of persons."—*Birmingham Journal*.

XXIV.

In 1 vol., price 10s. 6d.

GHOST STORIES,

BY CATHARINE CROWE,

Author of "Night Side of Nature."

"Mrs. Crowe's volume will delight the lovers of the supernatural, and their name is legion,"—*Morning Post.*

"These Tales are calculated to excite all the feelings of awe, and we may say of terror, with which Ghost Stories have ever been read."—*Morning Advertiser.*

XXV.

In 2 vols. post 8vo.

TEA TABLE TALK,

BY MRS. MATHEWS.

"Livingstone's Africa, and Mrs. Mathews' Tea Table Talk will be the two most popular works of the season."—*Bicester Herald.*

"It is ordinary criticism to say of a good gossiping book, that it is a volume for the sea-side, or for the fireside, or wet weather, or for a sunny nook, or in a shady grove, or for after dinner over wine and walnuts. Now these lively, gossiping volumes will be found adapted to all these places, times, and circumstances. They are brimfull of anecdotes. There are pleasant little biographical sketches and ambitious essays."—*Athenæum.*

"The anecdotes are replete with point and novelty and truthfullness."—*Sporting Magazine.*

"No better praise can be given by us than to say, that we consider this work one of, if not the most agreeable books that has come under our notice."—*Guardian.*

"For Book Clubs and Reading Societies no work can be found that will prove more agreeable."—*Express.*

"The widow of the late, and the mother of the present Charles Mathews would, under any circumstances, command our respect, and if we could not conscientiously praise her work, we should be slow to condemn it. Happily, however, the volumes in question are so good, that in giving this our favourable notice we are only doing justice to the literary character of the writer; her anecdotes are replete with point and novelty and truthfulnes that stamps them genuine."—*Sporting Review.*

XXVI.

In 2 vols., post 8vo., price 21s.

TWO JOURNEYS TO JAPAN,

BY KINAHAN CORNWALLIS.

"The mystery of Japan melts away as we follow Mr. Cornwallis. He enjoyed most marvellous good fortune, for he carried a spell with him which dissipated Japanese suspicion and procured him all sorts of privileges. His knowledge of Japan is considerable, It is an amusing Book."—*Athenaeum.*

"This is an amusing book, pleasantly written, and evidencing generous feeling."—*Literary Gazette.*

"We can honestly recommend Mr. Cornwallis's book to our readers."—*Morning Herald.*

"The country under his pencil comes out fresh, dewy, and picturesque before the eye. The volumes are full of amusement, lively and graphic."—*Chambers' Journal.*

XXVII.

In 1 vol., price 5s.

THINGS WORTH KNOWING ABOUT HORSES.

BY HARRY HIEOVER.

"From the days of Nimrod until now no man has made so many, few more valuable additions to what may be called 'Sporting Literature.' To those skilled in horses this litttle volume will be very welcome, whilst to the raw youth its teachings will be as precious as refined gold."—*Critic.*

"Into this little volume Harry Hieover has contrived to cram an innumerable quantity of things worth knowing about the tricks and bad habits of all kinds of horses, harness, starting, shying, and trotting; about driving; about the treatment of ailing horses; about corns, peculiarities of shape and make; and about stables, training, and general treatment."—*Field.*

"It is a useful hand-book about horses."—*Daily Telegraph.*

"Few men have produced better works upon the subject of horses than Harry Hieover."—*Review.*

"The author has omitted nothing of interest in his 'Things worth knowing about horses.'"—*Athenaeum.*

XXVIII.

In 1 vol. post 8vo., price 10s. 6d.

HISTORICAL GLEANINGS AT HOME AND ABROAD,

BY MRS. JAMIESON.

"This work is characterized by forcible and correct descriptions of men and manners in bygone years. It is replete with passages of the deepest interest."—*Review.*

XXIX.

In 1 vol. demy 8vo., price 12s.

THE SPORTSMAN'S FRIEND IN A FROST.

BY HARRY HIEOVER.

"Harry Hieover's practical knowledge and long experience in field sports, render his writings ever amusing and instructive. He relates most pleasing anecdotes of flood and field, and is well worthy of study."—*The Field.*

"No sportsman's library should be without it."—*Sporting Magazine.*

"There is amusement as well as intelligence in Harry Hieover's book."—*Athenaeum.*

XXX.

In 1 vol. demy 8vo., price 12s.

SPORTING FACTS & SPORTING FANCIES.

BY HARRY HIEOVER.

Author of "Stable Talk and Table Talk," "The Pocket and the Stud," "The Hunting Field," &c.

"This work will make a valuable and interesting addition to the sportsman's library."—*Bell's Life.*

"In addition to the immense mass of practical and useful information with which this work abounds, there is a refreshing buoyancy and dash about the style, which makes it as attractive and fascinating as the pages of the renowned Nimrod himself."—*Dispatch.*

"It contains graphic sketches of celebrated young sporting characters."—*Sunday Times.*

XXXI.

In 1 vol., price 5s.

THE SPORTING WORLD.

BY HARRY HIEOVER.

"Reading Harry Hieover's book is like listening lazily and luxuriously after dinner to a quiet gentlemanlike, clever talker."—*Athenaeum.*

"It will be perused with pleasure by all who take an interest in the manly game of our fatherland. It ought to be added to every sportsman's library."—*Sporting Review.*.

XXXII.

FOURTH EDITION, PRICE 5s.

THE PROPER CONDITION OF ALL HORSES.

BY HARRY HIEOVER.

"It should be in the hands of all owners of horses."—*Bell's Life.*

"A work which every owner of a horse will do well to consult."—*Morning Herald.*

"Every man who is about purchasing a horse, whether it be hunter, riding-horse, lady's palfrey, or cart-horse, will do well to make himself acquainted with the contents of this book."—*Sporting Magazine.*

XXXIII.

In 1 vol., price 5s.

HINTS TO HORSEMEN,

SHOWING HOW TO MAKE MONEY BY HORSES.

BY HARRY HIEOVER.

"When Harry Hieover gives hints to Horseman, he does not mean by that term riders exclusively, but owners, breeders, buyers, sellers, and admirers of horses. To teach such men how to make money is to impart no valuless instruction to a large class of mankind. The advice is frankly given, and if no benefit result, it will not be for the want of good counsel."—*Athenaeum.*

"It is by far the most useful and practical book that Harry Hieover has written."—*Express.*

XXXIV.

In 1 vol. price 5s.

THE WORLD AND HOW TO SQUARE IT.

BY HARRY HIEOVER.

XXXV.

In 1 vol., price 4s.

BIPEDS AND QUADRUPEDS,

BY HARRY HIEOVER.

"We recommend this little volume for the humanity towards quadrupeds it advocates, and the proper treatment of them that it inculcates."—*Bell's Life.*

XXXVI.

In 2 vols. post 8vo., price 21s.

NAPLES,

POLITICAL, SOCIAL, AND RELIGIOUS.

BY LORD B*****

"The pictures are as lively and bright as the colours and climate they reflect."—*Spectator.*

"It is a rapid, clear historical sketch."—*Advertiser.*

"The author has done good service to society."—*Court Circular.*

XXXVII.

In 2 vols., price 21s., cloth.

THE LIFE OF PERCY BYSSHE SHELLY.

BY CAPTAIN MEDWIN,

Author of "Conversations with Lord Byron."

"This book must be read by every one interested in literature."—*Morning Post.*

"A complete life of Shelley was a desideratum in literature and there was no man so competent as Captain Medwin to supply it."—*Inquirer.*

"The book is sure of exciting much discussion."—*Literary Gazette.*

XXXVIII.

Price 1s. 6d.

PRINCE LIFE.

BY G. P. R. JAMES, ESQ.,

Author of "The Gipsy," "Richelieu," &c.

"It is worth its weight in gold."—"*The Globe.*"

"Most valuable to the rising generation; an invaluable little book."—*Guardian.*

XXXIX.

Second Edition, now ready, in 3 vols., price 42s.

THE LITERARY LIFE AND CORRESPONDENCE

OF THE

COUNTESS OF BLESSINGTON.

BY R. MADDEN, Esq., F.R.C.S.-ENG.

Author of "Travels in the East," "Life of Savonarola," &c.

"We may, with perfect truth affirm that during the last fifty years there has been no book of such peculiar interest to the literary and political world. It has contributions from every person of literary reputation—Byron, Sir E. Bulwer, who contributes an original Poem, James, D'Israeli, Marryatt, Savage Landor, Campbell, L. E. L., the Smiths, Shelley, Jenkyn, Sir W. Gell, Jekyll, &c., &c.; as well as letters from the most eminent Statesmen and Foreigners of distinction, the Duke of Wellington, Marquis Wellesley, Marquis Douro, Lords Lyndhurst, Brougham, Durham, Abinger, &c."—*Morning Post.*

XL.

In 1 vol., price 7s. 6d.

ON SEX IN THE WORLD TO COME.

BY THE REV. G. B. HAUGHTON, A.M.

"A peculiar subject; but a subject of great interest, and in this volume treated in a masterly style. The language is surpassingly good, showing the author to be a learned and a thoughtful man."—*New Quarterly Review.*

XLI.

Price 2s. 6d. beautifully illustrated.

THE HAPPY COTTAGE,

A TALE FOR SUMMER'S SUNSHINE.

By the Author of "Kate Vernon," "Agness Waring."

XLII.

In I vol. 8vo.

THE AGE OF PITT AND FOX.

BY DANIEL OWEN MADDEN,

Author of "Chiefs of Party," &c.

The *Times* says "We may safely pronounce it to be the best text-book of the age which it professes to describe."

XLIII.

In 3 vols. demy 8vo., price 2l. 14s.

A CATHOLIC HISTORY OF ENGLAND.

BY W. MAC CABE, Esq.

"A work of great literary value."—*Times.*

XLIV.

In 1 vol., price 14s.

LIVES OF THE PRIME MINISTERS OF ENGLAND.

FROM THE RESTORATION TO THE PRESENT TIME.

BY J. HOUSTON BROWN, L.L.B.

Of the Inner Temple, Barrister-at-Law.

"The Biographer has collected the facts relating to the family and career of his four subjects, Clarendon, Clifford, Danby and Essex, and stated these facts with clearness;—selected such personal traits as the memoirs and lampoons of the time have presented, and interspersed his biographies with passing notices of the times and reflections, which though sometimes harsh in character or questionable in taste, have independence, and, at all events, a limited truth."—*Spectator.*

XLV.

In 2 vols., price 10s.

SHELLEY AND HIS WRITINGS.

BY C. S. MIDDLETON, Esq.

"Never was there a more perfect specimen of biography."— *Walter Savage Landor, Esq.*

"Mr. Middleton has done good service. He has carefully sifted the sources of information we have mentioned, has made some slight addition, and arranged his materials in proper order and in graceful language. It is the first time the mass of scattered information has been collected, and the ground is therefore cleared for the new generation of readers."—*Athenaeum.*

"The Life of the Poet which has just appeared, and which was much required, is written with much beauty of expression and clearness of purpose. Mr. Middleton's book is a masterly performance."—*Somerset Gazette.*

"Mr. Middleton has displayed great ability in following the poet through all the mazes of his life and thoughts. We recommend the work as lively, animated and interesting. It contains many curious disclosures."—*Sunday Times.*

XLVI.

In 1 vol., price 1s. 6d.

THE FIRST LATIN COURSE

BY REV. J. ARNOLD.

"For beginners, this Latin Grammar is unequalled."—*Scholastic.*

XLVII.

Price 7s. 6d.

INDIAN RELIGIONS,

By a Missionary.

XLVIII.

NEW FRENCH GRAMMAR,

Price 3s; 6d.

LE TRESOR DE LA LANGUE FRANCAISE,

Comprising French and English Exercises, a recueil of Sentences, Proverbs, Dialogues, and Anecdotes, forming a Reading book, terminated by a French and English Dictionary.

BY C. A. DE G. LIANCOURT, M.A.

Professor of Compared Languages.

"This Grammar will be used in every school in England. It is an invaluable assistant to masters, and facilitates the acquisition of the language to the pupil without fatiguiug with a multiplicity of rules."—*The Scholastic.*

POPULAR
NEW NOVELS.

....

I.

In 3 vols. post 8vo., price £1 11s. 6d.

THE STORY OF A LOST LIFE,

By W. PLATT,

Author of "Betty Westminster."

"Mr. Platt has evidently taken great pains and bestowed much thought on this novel, and the result is, he has given us the most charming piece of nature-painting we have read for many a day."—*Globe.*

II.

In 1 vol., price 10s. 6d.

MANORDEAN.

III.

In 3 vols. post 8vo. price £3 11s. 6d.

TRIED IN THE FIRE,

BY MRS. MACKENZIE DANIELS,

Author of "My Sister Minnie," "Our Guardian," &c.

"Mrs. Mackenzie Daniels, whose tales have gained for her considerable reputation as a novelist has, under this suggestive title, given us a story of exquisite beauty. The characters are as life-like as it is possible to immagine. For graceful language and the high moral it inculcates, there will be few better novels published this season."—*Globe.*

IV.

In 2 vols. post 8vo. price £1 11s. 6d.

THE GREAT EXPERIMENT,

BY MISS MOLESWORTH,

Author of "The Stumble on the Threshold," &c.

"The Great Experiment, consists in pointing out to the world the evils arising from ill-assorted marriages, and we venture to predict that it will attain a degree of celebrity that will not be surpassed by any other novel in the year 1860."— *Globe.*

"Lessons of something more valuable than those of worldly wisdom can be gathered from Miss Molesworth's novel. The married may find how to render their state permanently happy —those about to marry, are told with what feelings they should enter upon their new duties, and those who are seeking husbands and wives will do well to study and ponder Miss Molesworth's axioms in the 'The Great Experiment.' "—*Guardian.*

"A powerful and correct delineator of character and an originality of thought and expression."—*Court Journal.*

V.

In 3 vols. price £1 11s. 6d.

COUNTRY LANDLORDS,

By L. M. S.

"Author of Gladys of Harloch."

VI ·

In 2 vols. price 21s.

Coming Events Cast their Shadows Before,

"A more lively and loveable character than Constance presents is rarely conceived. The language throughout is unusually pure and worthy of the subject."—*Globe.*

VII.

In 2 vols. post 8vo. price £1 11s. 6d.

SYBIL GREY.

"Sybil Grey is a novel to be read by a mother to a daughter, or by a father to the loved circle at the domestic fireside."—*Herald.*

VIII.

In 3 vols. post 8vo. price £1 11s. 6d.

THE HOME AND THE PRIEST,

BY SIGNOR VOLPE.

" It peculiarly illustrates the spirit and motives of the present movement in Italy, especially in exposing, by the force of a personal story, that intolerable, corrupt, and corrupting tyrany, which the Roman priesthood exercises alike over the commonwealth and the home."—*Globe.*

"The author relies, with reason, upon the universal interest now felt in all that relates to Italy. The work portrays the crimes, intrigues, cruelty and treachery of the tonsured orders, and it is wrought out with considerable skill."—*Athenæum.*

" The actual working of the Italian church system is shown not only in relation to the Italian's private home, but in relation also to his country. Sig. Volpe sees no hope for Italy, but in the uprooting of the spiritual as well as temporal dominions of the Pope."—*Examiner.*

" The machinations of priestcraft, the unscrupulous tendencies of Popery are here laid down with a vigorous and an usurping hand. These volumes afford a broad picture of Italian social and political life."—*Dispatch.*

" It is admirably written and abounds in vivid representation of strong passion."—*Guardian.*

IX.

In 2 vols. price 21s. Second Edition.

MABEL OWEN.

" A novel it is a pleasure to read, and what is better a novel, it is a pleasure to reflect on after reading."—*Scottish Press.*

"Actions and feelings are delineated with such truthfulness as give evidence of a remarkable and minute observer of the writings of a woman's heart. It is written for the best purpose a novelist can employ his pen."—*Leader.*

" The best novel of the season."—*Advertiser.*

" There is no individual whose history and private experience, if honestly and freely told, would not be interesting, and we can truly say this of the present work."—*Express.*

X.

In 1 vol. post 8vo. price 10s. 6d.

(Second Edition.)

MY VILLAGE NEIGHBOURS,

BY MISS G. M. STERNE.

" This Tale will prove a most agreeable companion for the long winter evenings. We have not read anything equal to it since the Publication of Miss Mitford's ' Our Village' which it much resembles."—*Scotch Press.*

"Miss Sterne writes agreeably and with facility after the fashion of Miss Mitford."—*Athenæum.*

"There is a great deal of power in these volumes—the author possesses a very unusual command of language and a rare degree of pathos."—*Morning Herald.*

"The style is rustic, simple and thoroughly entertaining. Miss Sterne is the Great Cousin of Lawrence Sterne the author of "The Sentimental Journey," and bids fair not to diminish the illustrious name she bears."—*Court Journal.*

" Contains pleasing sketches of country scenery and agreeable details of the varieties of character proper to such a locality."—*Globe.*

XI.

In 2 vols. post 8vo. price 21s.

HONESTY IS THE BEST POLICY,

By Mrs. AUGUSTUS PEEL.

" Mrs. Agustus Peel has worked out this Proverb admirably in her new novel under that Title, and it is a pleasure to find that her book is in every way worthy the name she bears. The language is eloquent, the style unaffected and the story interesting from begining to end."—*Globe.*

"A very pleasing and instructive novel."—*Atlas.*

XII.

In 3 vols., price 31s. 6d.

MASTER AND PUPIL,

By Mrs. MACKENZIE DANIELS.

XIII.

In 3 vols. post 8vo. price £1 11s. 6d.

THE LILY OF DEVON,

BY C. F. ARMSTRONG.

"This is chiefly a naval novel, and it is long since we have met with one so deserving of notice."—*Naval and Military.*

"It is a capital book of its class and may be recommended as one likely to prove highly acceptable to novel reading."—*Morning Post.*

"The author is a disciple of Captain Marryatt's. His work is clever and dashing."—*Oriental Budget.*

XIV.

In 1 vol., price 7s. 6d.

MILLY WARRENER.

"A pleasant, unpretending story; it is a life-like story of a young country girl more refined than her station. There are incidental sketches of country characters which are clever and spirited."—*Athenæum.*

XV.

In 2 vols., price 21s.

THE COUNT DE PERBRUCK,

By HENRY COOKE, Esq.

"A tale of the Vendean war, invested with a new interest. Mr. Cooke has done his part most successfully. His vivid, graphic colouring and well-chosen incidents prove him a master in the art of historical delineation."—*Guardian.*

"Of Mr. Cooke's share in the work we can speak with deserved approbation."—*Press.*

"It has the merit of keeping alive the excitement of the reader till the closing page."—*Morning Post.*

"This highly-interesting romance will find a place amongst the standard works of fiction."—*Family Herald.*

"This is an experiment, and a successful one."—*Atlas.*

XVI.

In 3 vol., price 31s. 6d.

THE CAMPBELLS,

"The story is full of interest."—*Enquirer.*

XVII.

In 3 vols., price 31s. 6d.

EBB AND FLOW.

"It will amuse thos who like to find something out of the usual even tenor of a novel; to such it can fairly be recommended."—*The Sun.*

XVIII.

In 3 vols., price 31s. 6d.

GEORGIE BARRINGTON,

By the Author of "Old Memories," &c.

"This novel is full of power, full of interest, and full of those fascinations and spells which none but extraordinarily-gifted can produce."—*Globe.*

XIX.

In 2 vols., price 21s.

BEVERLEY PRIORY.

"This is an admirable tale."—*Naval and Military.*

"Beverley Priory is in no part of it a dull novel, and is unquestionably clever."—*Examiner.*

XX

In 3 vols., price 31s. 6d.

THE PARSON AND THE POOR.

" There is much that is very good in this tale ; it is cleverly written, and with good feeling."—*Athenæum*.

" We have read this novel with a great deal of pleasure ; the dialogue is always spirited and natural. The children talk like children, and the men and women remind us of flesh and blood." —*Morning Herald*.

" The characters and incidents are such as will live in the memory of the reader, while the style and spirit of the book will render it not only pleasant but profitable reading."— *Bradford Review*.

" The author has made the incidents of every-day life a vehicle through which lessons of virtue, blended with religion, may be conveyed."—*Kilkenny Moderator*.

" A story of country life, written by one who knew well how to describe both cottage and hall life."—

" It bears the impress of truth and Nature's simplicity throughout."—*Illustrated News of the World*.

XXI.

In 3 vols., price 31s. 6d.

THE FATE OF FOLLY,

BY LORD B*******

Author of Masters and Workmen, &c.

" This is one of the very few works of fiction that should be added to every Public Free Library. It contains more moral lessons, more to elevate the minds of readers, and has higher aims than almost any novel we have read. At the same time, it is replete with incident and amusement."—*Globe*.

" It is a good book."—*Spectator*.

XXII.

In 3 vols., price 31s. 6d.

BETTY WESTMINSTER,

BY W. PLATT, Esq.

"A lesson of sound practical morality, inculcated with charming effect;—a story which bears in every chapter the impress of intellect, taste, and sensibility."—*Morning Post.*

"Betty Westminster is the representative of a type of society but little used by novelists—the money-getting tradesmen of provincial towns. It is written with talent and considerable skill."— *New Quarterly Review.*

"There is a great deal of cleverness in this story."—*Examiner.*

"There is much comic satire in it. The author has power worth cultivating "—*Examiner.*

"There is a good deal of spirit in these volumes, and great talent shown in the book "—*Athenæum.*

"A book of greater interest has not come under our notice for years."—*Review.*

"All is described by a master hand."—*John Bull.*

XXIII.

In 3 vols., post 8vo., 31s. 6d.

FROM THE PEASANTRY TO THE PEERAGE.

BY BLUE TUNIC.

XXIV.

In 2 vols., post 8vo., price 21s.

THE TWO HOUSEHOLDS.

www.ingramcontent.com/pod-product-compliance
Lightning Source LLC
Chambersburg PA
CBHW020856020726
47497CB00005B/1438